The Unpu

By Kayl

Contents

It was a quaint Thursday in January when Helen's life ended. She had had an argument with her mother regarding a set of curtains that she had ordered for her living room. Her mother had kept her on the phone for a good twenty minutes, complaining that she had spent too much money on the fabric and that Helen wasn't adequately saving for her future.

Due to the heated conversation and Helen's subsequent mood, she had decided not to visit her parents as she normally did on a Tuesday, as she believed that a 24-hour cooling off period was called for.

She skipped her morning shower; after remembering that she had a bath bomb still to use and thought that it would be a nice treat for her at the end of what she believed would be a very long day. As Helen worked from home; she could wear anything.... including a bikini. This she had donned a couple of summers ago, when temperatures reached record levels. Helen couldn't wear any more clothes when working in her home office, for fear of cooking her internal organs. She normally threw on whatever was at the front of her wardrobe, usually joggers that were too crummy to be worn outside.

But today, instead of sitting in her usual joggers and pink slippers, she put on her polka-dot playsuit that was bright and fluffy, and sat down to work. Helen's office was the second bedroom of her two up, two down, end of terrace cottage. The room was painted bright yellow, with a white board across the length of one of the walls. It had lots of scribbles on it that made complete sense to Helen; however, if anyone else looked at it, they would have thought it was some 'Alan Turing' work, instead of a breakdown of the new project she was close to completing.

The smell of the coffee lingered through the house as she got out her work book. The sun was shining in to the hall and reflected off the small mirror in Helen's office. Having been working at her desk for about twenty minutes, she had finally stopped replaying the argument that she had had with her mother over and over again in her head.

Helen could never concentrate in silence, always needing some background noise to allow her to focus, so it was normal to hear the radio in the corner of her office when she was working. When the radio stopped blaring out its usual auto tuned new pop group that was taking the nation by storm, it crackled.....

Mayday, Mayday 482 heavy requesting immediate landing. Mayday, Mayday. 482 heavy we have total electrical failures and need to land.

The voice was male and sounded extremely distressed. Helen's whole body tensed up, her hand frozen holding a pencil that had been drawing a foundation line just seconds earlier. Helen was an architect and was working on a design for a new inner-city health care centre; it was her first big responsibility, that she was taking very seriously. She had lived over a flight path for the past three years and had gotten used to the planes landing at all times of the day and night. She hadn't taken a breath since the last crackle of her radio which kept talking to her.

Control, I repeat we have complete electrical failure. Can anyone hear me?

Helen hadn't heard a response from air traffic control or anyone else. Picking up a small amount of radio chatter was normal for her and happened a couple of times a month. It had been explained to Helen, that the reason was due to the flight path of the planes and the location of the radio relay tower. An explanation that she hadn't really understood, however, she just nodded, otherwise she would have had it explained to her again.

Helen hadn't moved since the radio crackled and she started to panic. Her body went cold with a wash of sweat, the fluffy playsuit became prickly on her skin. Had anyone heard what had happened? Was anyone helping the plane? How big was the plane? Was it full? Helen just sat there, her pencil still in the exact same place, unmoving, listening to the radio, with all the will in the world to hear another voice, another voice say, 'We got you. We can help'. Another crackle

Mayday, Mayday this is 482 heavy can anyone....?

Then the radio crackled and a classic hit from the 1990's was introduced by the disc jockey, before it started its slow drawl about love and loss.

Helen sat there, still, silent. Not a muscle in her body was moving. Everything was the same as it had been 20 minutes before, except she was no longer holding her pencil. That had rolled off the table, out of the open door to the office and was now resting on the cream carpet in the hallway.
Helen had had a heart attack and had died then and there, listening to the distress of the captain over the radio. Her body was still rigid, the hair that had fallen in front of her eyes was still there. She sat motionless, suspended in time, waiting to be found. The dryer beeped to indicate that the cycle had finished and needed to be unloaded while it was hot, before it started to crease. But there was no one there to hear the beep. Helen was never going to wear those clothes again, so it didn't really matter if they were creased or not. There was a black cat scratching at the back door in want of attention and the drawl, coming out of the radio, had finished and was currently being referred to as a classic.

Briar paused over her laptop. Her brain was whirling with thoughts. She checked the wall clock in her living room, that was over the mantel piece. It was 5am. Briar had been unable to get back to sleep at 3am, after cleaning the oven in her kitchen. So, she sat on the floor, in front of her coffee table in her living room, turned to her laptop and began to write. She had been writing the life of Helen for the last two hours and was honestly shocked with herself that she had just killed off her main character. Briar had been plotting the story for a couple of weeks, while at work. However, the idea to kill her had not been in Briar's notes and she sat there looking at the screen, not knowing where to possibly take the story now that her main character was dead in chapter three.

Briar glanced at the clock again. It was still 5am. She knew that her bedside alarm clock would be going off in fifteen minutes and, despite having only had three hours sleep, she felt very awake. She looked over the chapter that she had just written. She knew that this was a first draft and that she would have to go back and add in description and some better punctuation. Briar could see Helen in her mind's eye, sitting at her desk. She was wearing her fluffy polka dot playsuit. She had dark brown hair, tied in a loose ponytail, half of her hair had fallen in front of her face. Helen had well shaped eyebrows and rosy cheeks. The most unusual thing about Helen was that, even though she had dark hair, her green eyes were framed by thin blonde eye lashes. Briar liked that little detail. When working from home, Helen never bothered with makeup and the lack of applying it every day was evident in such healthy, spot free skin. She had been sitting on a cheap fold out chair and there was a cup of apricot tea cooling next to her. When Briar was writing she always ended up adding in a cup of her favourite type of tea or a slice of cake. Briar stared at her laptop, deep in thought; trying to decide to adapt the plot of her story to fit within the parameters of the last scene or to completely abandon the new scene, that had made her tear up whilst writing it.

Briar's thoughts turned to the reason Helen could have died, Heart attack? Shock? Can people really die from shock? She looked over and searched with her eyes the bookshelf behind her television for her dad's medical book. She wondered if there was anything documented on what condition could have killed her. But the thought of looking through the book now seemed exhausting. Briar didn't have any of her Dad's possessions other than the book and a couple of photographs. Everything else had been thrown in the skip the day they had buried him. When Briar's dad had killed himself, her mother had seen it as an abandonment. After the reading of the will and a quick funeral, she was never allowed to speak of her father again.

Briar jumped when her alarm started quacking at her. She quickly saved her work, both to the laptop and the USB stick that lived in the small monkey nuts pot on the coffee table, and shut her computer. As she got up, she tied her hair in to a bun on the top of her head, stretching her back as she did and letting out a loud yawn. By the time she had made it to her bedside and turned off the alarm, she was completely naked. She always thought that quacking ducks sounded like they were laughing and the idea of ducks chuckling to themselves to wake her up in the morning was something that she liked. Briar threw her bed clothes on to her pillow, remade her barely slept in double bed and headed for the bathroom. Not being a lady that messed about, she was in the shower, out and dressed before 5.38AM Applying a light dusting of make up in front of her hall mirror, she headed off down the stairs to work.

Briar's hall mirror was her favourite piece of furniture. She called it her Mirror Mirror' mirror. It reminded her of the mirror that the evil queen had in the fairy tale that her Mother used to tell her when she was young. With an intricate iron frame, Briar kept her hair bobbles on the edges. In front of the mirror, on the small glass table top next to the bowl of her make-up, she had a candle that looked like the rosy apple with which the Evil Queen tempted the Princess. The flame on the candle was supposed to burn black, however, Briar didn't want to ruin, it by lighting it

As she got to the bottom of the stairs, that connected the flat to the shop below. Briar reached up to the top of the door frame. She pulled the key that was hanging on a pulley chord, and unlocked the connecting door, letting the key go, it slowly wound up on the string and came to rest back at the top of the door frame, just as Briar shut the door behind her. She used her keys that were attached to her belt to lock the door from the kitchen side. Kicking off her fluffy pink slippers, with a hole in the toe, she fished under the island and slipped on her blue flats that had been discarded there the night before. As she walked through the yellow shop kitchen, she could see Cleo, her tortoiseshell cat, with a fabulously silver sparkly collar, walking the tightrope over the mantelpiece. Briar had taken some decisive action when Cleo had showed up at the kitchen door, the year before, with her spotted handkerchief and with her big eyes and cute head tilt, and asked to live with Briar.

Briar had stuck the candle to the mantelpiece, with double strength glue, and prayed that she didn't fall out of love with them. As they would be near impossible to remove.

As Briar watched the nimble feline curl her tail around the two small tea lights and gently jump on to the nearest leather armchair, she turned on all the appliances in the small kitchen. The only things she left on overnight were the two fridges. She pulled her hair tighter and headed through the kitchen door frame, out to the front counter and in to her tea shop. The tea shop had lilac walls and a white skirting board. The bay sash windows had bold orange pillows on them, there were twenty or so mismatched armchairs and sofas that were grouped around differently shaded wooden tables, that had jars of white and brown sugar on them. The wooden floor was covered in mismatched rugs of different patterns and hid the stained floor from when she tried to tie dye some tablecloths and knocked over the dye. It had turned half of the lovely floor a strange black colour and didn't look very professional. The idea of buying lots of cheap rugs to try and hide them in the short term; that had paid off the day after they were delivered. One of Briar's customers, Martin, had a fit and wasn't wearing his helmet. The rugs stopped him from smacking his head on the hard floor and Briar kept them. Despite the snide remarks from the local middle-aged ladies, the character it added to her little slice of heaven, was something that Briar enjoyed and reminded her that it was her decision as to what would happen with her shop and no one was able to tell her what to do.

Briar opened the front door to the teashop, to collect the milk that had been left there by Jack half an hour earlier. There was a pint of semi skimmed milk in a glass bottle, lying next to the bottle was a single yellow rose. It was 6.15am and the official start of her day.

She picked up both items with her right hand, the smile radiating from cheek to cheek as she admired the rose; It smelled sweet and fresh, having been clipped from a rose bush that morning. It was Monday and today the milk bottle had the letter 'O' written in Black pen. In all the years that she had been collecting the milk from the front of the shop she had never understood what the letters were for. All she knew was that there was a different one every day. Had Briar thought about it she would have used it as a talking point with Jack, the milkman; when he would pop in to the shop the first Thursday of every month to collect payment for the milk.

Briar thought about Jack for a second; he was just shy of 6 feet tall, with sandy blonde hair that was cut short at the sides. He was always freshly shaven and had a swimmer's body. When he was nervous he used to rub his thumb and little finger together. He wore black trainers and loose blue jeans. His v neck shirts always fitted perfectly. He had a small mole just under his left eye and a birth mark on the side of his neck that his sister insisted was a miniature version of the map of the United States of America. Jack had served for 7 years in the Royal Marines and had been honourably discharged, when a grenade exploded near to him and he lost a large proportion of his hearing in his left ear.

Briar thought that Jack had made his intentions clear in the roses, but she also had never had the courage to pursue the relationship, even though she desperately wanted Jack to ask her out. So, she continued to collect roses from him and in turn leave him loose tea leaves wrapped in crape paper with the empty milk bottles. The leaves for the next day had already been wrapped up in the white crape paper, with a gold ribbon tied into two small bows. The precious cargo this time was apricot tea, one of Briar's favourites, and she would leave it ready for Jack at the end of the day, along with the empty milk bottle ready for the pick up the next morning. One pint of milk a day was not nearly enough to supply the stream of customers that Briar served every day. The pint that Jack dropped off was just for Briar to use in the numerous cakes she made every day. Briar also liked the fact that she was supporting the local farmers by buying from the milkman.

Briar knew that she couldn't afford to dawdle today and pushed the thoughts of Jack to the back of her mind, focusing on her morning routine. Her planned 90 minutes break where she shut the teashop after lunch, before the after-school run was today being taken up by reading through the CVs for the interviews for the new weekend waitress that she had scheduled for tomorrow. But as that wasn't until the afternoon, she had a lot of things to do before then. One of Briar's rules was to try and keep work downstairs and not let it seep in to her evenings, a rule that she broke most days. The last thing she wanted was to be eating her dinner at 9pm and working. Especially on days when she didn't shut the shop at all.

Closing the front door, the echo of the smile from the rose still on her face, Briar turned took a deep breath and launched gracefully into her day. There was a solitary teacup on the table nearest the counter, having been left there the night before. She scooped it up, as she headed around the counter and in to the kitchen. It was a very graceful move, as if she was skating on a frozen lake. The muscle memory of doing it thousands of times was evident, but went unnoticed as she was alone in the shop. She entered the kitchen and was met by the familiar smell of desiccated coconut. Placing the glass milk bottle on the central counter, she popped the yellow rose in the purple chipped vase, that lived above the old fridge. There were six roses now in the vase, all different colours and different stages of life. Briar's bunch of roses were ever changing, with Jack bringing her a different colour flower with every bottle. The oldest rose had been a blood orange colour; however, it now had only the faintest traces of orange and better resembled a mud brown rose, still beautiful, having aged but was not long for the bin.

Briar looked around her teashop and smiled. She loved what she had accomplished since inheriting it from her Mother. Who had been out at the local shop, picking up something for dinner when she had a heart attack in the cheese aisle and died on the way to hospital in an ambulance. Two police officers had been sent to inform Briar of what had happened. She had been carrying a pot of tea, which she had dropped on the floor when she was told the news. There is still a dent in the floor where the teapot shattered. Whenever Briar treads on the floor just right she can feel the dent through her crocs and she feels like her heart jumps out of her chest for a fraction of a second. As if her heart remembered that feeling of loss again and again. One thing Briar regretted about her and Rose's relationship, was that she couldn't remember the last thing that her mother had said to her, before she had left for the shops.

Once the funeral service had finished and the tissues used to dab away the tears had been thrown away and she had finally said goodbye to the last mourner. Locking the front door to the teashop, she had cut up all the flowery cushions and ripped down the pale pink wallpaper before then sun had gone down. The next morning, she had taken down the old sign above the door and had painted the old pale pink window frames. All aspects of anything frilly had been discarded or destroyed. The laced tablecloths were in the bin. The ornaments doted on the tables in a card board box near the front door ready to go to the charity shops and the doilies now resembled a box of confetti.

Many things had changed after the funeral and, in the seventeen months since her mother's death, Briar had been discovering things that she could now do. Before then she would have never been allowed to keep roses from the milkman or put the damp tea towels on the counter top. God forbid she had even changed something as small as the teaspoons or the type of sugar that is served with the tea and hot coffee; as ice coffee was also not an option. Now however she served a variety of both iced coffee and iced teas to the delight of her younger clients. The investment in an ice cream maker was also evident of the changed menu, since the Tea Shop had received a complete overhaul. Briar having worked there every day for the past fifteen years ever since her fourteenth birthday and her mother insisting that she would have to start earning her keep.

The Unpublished Tea Shop, as it was now called, had previously been called Roses Tea Shop. Rose had inherited the shop from her aunt, also a traditionalist, also called Rose. Technically it was Rosemary, but only her husband called her that; who wanted to run a nice establishment where doctors and vicars' wives could meet to discuss the local gossip that was circulating the town that week. Roses Tea Shop had quickly turned in to the gossip location to discuss the scandalous events of the week, such as who had not washed their curtains or who had not kept their garden up to scratch. Occasionally there would be a big scandal, which increased Rose's takings for the week.

For example, when Mr and Mrs Monterosso had moved in to the town. They had arrived from Italy and had decided to throw a dinner party to try and get to know their new neighbours. They invited the local bank manager, Mr Hollis, and his wife to dinner. Instead of a traditional meal such as pie and mash or sausages casserole, Mr and Mrs Hollis had been presented with spaghetti and meatballs; a truly foreign food. The Monterosso's had been a lovely couple but the embarrassment of serving that at dinner and the gossip that followed meant they had been shunned in the town and left four months later for a better life in America. That was way back in 1936 and the little town had come on since then, but not by much. Briar's teashop had undergone such a transformation that Briar hoped that her mother, Rose, and her great aunt, Rose, were both turning in their graves with all the changes that she had implemented. Besides the furniture and the menu, the main difference was the three large mahogany bookcases that stood separately in the three corners of the shop and were a vital part of the new name.

The Unpublished Tea Shop was precisely that, a shop where people could come in and stay for as long as they liked, to read a book, that was not available on mass, as the authors were unpublished - an opportunity to have something that was completely unique, to sit in one of the eleven crushed velvet arm chairs or the three sofas and lose themselves in a story. The idea of the unpublished tea shop had taken hold years earlier. Briar was a writer - well she wanted to be a writer. She had studied English literature at university and dreamt of sitting on a beach writing her novel and had completed around fifteen short stories, however, she had never had any luck in getting any of them published. So, one Saturday evening while her mother still had control of the shop, after all the pots had been washed and the tables wiped down, Briar had decided to print off all her stories and bind them in to books and leaving them in the shop for people to read at their leisure. She thought that she could get a bit of feedback on how to improve her writing and finally get a response from any of the publishing companies that she had bombarded with countless copies.

Rose, to Briar's surprise, had allowed a small bookshelf in her teashop and Briar left the copies of the short stories on there and had a very proud feeling when she placed all her literary works for anyone to read. The next week when a gentleman had gone over to sit in the tea shop for a couple of hours, as he had apparently arrived in the town early for a meeting one of the local businesses, he had picked up one of her stories named 'The White Parrot' and thoroughly enjoyed it.

The next week, when collecting the mail from the post office, Briar had received a large package from the same gentleman. It contained his first novel, along with a note saying that the idea of having books, that had failed to be published, available to the public to be a 'fabulous idea', and in wanting to be a part of it, sent a copy and a cheque for £20 to pay for the bookcase. Since then, he had sent her three following novels which, she regretfully did not enjoy, but believing people should always be given a chance, had put the books on the shelf for anyone to read. The gentleman had not been the only person to send in manuscripts. Word had spread and, in total, she had received around two hundred books. They were of all different shapes and sizes. She had accumulated around forty books before Roses death but the idea had really taken off, since the shop overhaul and the reputation of the unique teashop had begun to spread, both by word of mouth and on line. Briar had a diary on the fridge, next to the purple vase, that held the information of all the people who had given their scripts and any letters that had accompanied the submissions. There were a few anonymous submissions, but she put them out just the same, after having read them to ensure that they didn't contain anything that was inappropriate for the tea shop. She had refused one book, since taking in submissions and after a horrible conversation with a vile man who tried to bully her in to taking the book was unsuccessful. Briar viewed the interaction to be a complete victory as she had stood her ground and it had really been a jumping off point for the way that she was going to continue to live her life. Where in which she wasn't going to do anything that she didn't want to.

She also had written down all the correspondence from people online. She liked the idea of dipping in to other people's lives to a very subtle extent, a person being able to show you an accomplishment or a snippet from their life that had made them smile. She had about two hundred followers and followed a healthy ninety-seven individuals. One of them, however, always received more attention than the rest 'Jacktheready' was his screen name and he was Jack the milkman.

Briar put the milk on the counter and stood in front of her mum's old cook book. She took another deep breath, and got out the large mixing bowl and placed it next to the drying tea towel on the counter. She began to sift the flour through the sieve, tapping the side of the sieve with her open left palm. Briar was making a cheesecake for a 40th wedding anniversary the next day, a recipe that she used at least one a week. This recipe however had a slight twist on it. The couple wanted a mint cheesecake. Which is why Briar wanted to make it the day before, just in case it was a disaster and she could remake it if needed. She was a lady that liked to get all the baking done in the morning before she opened at 7 am. She had already slipped on the home-made apron, which held the only evidence of the night of passion that she had had with an old university friend and, after half a bottle of tequila and a lot of flirting they had ended up ripping off each other's clothes and getting down to business on the kitchen floor. In their haste to get undressed, the apron had been flung on the lit stove and the was a small circular hole that had been burnt through the cloth. Luckily there was no other damage and the escapade hadn't ended up with them standing outside the burning tea shop, with blankets, as firefighters dealt with the remains of the business. The price of the passion had mainly impacted the right pocket that still hadn't been repaired, and she could poke her finger through when she was standing with her hands in her pockets. Not that she had much time to stand around with her hands in her pockets, but it was also a nice reminder of a fabulous night.

Briar flicked on the kettle and the radio, which was always set to her favourite station and contemplated which tea to start with, as she measured the sugar in to three smaller mixing bowls. Rose's black recipe book open on the counter next to the kettle just in case she had to check the recipe. A nice little safety net that she never used but it was nice to have around.

From where Briar was standing, she could see through the teashop and out on to the street. She looked up and caught a glimpse of the back end of Jack's milk float. Briar automatically lengthened her neck to appear taller and slender and then noticed that she had been mixing with her tongue sticking out of her mouth. She hoped that Jack hadn't caught her looking stupid, as she cut up the strawberries for the ganache to go on the strawberry cheesecake.

CHAPTER 2

Briar sat on a stool in her kitchen. It was 6.45am, and the three cheesecakes were cooling on the wire racks, positioned in front of the ice cream maker. She was making sugar flowers to be placed on the range of cakes, that had been ordered by Mrs Hollis Jr. for her annual September party on Saturday. Briar hated the woman, she lived at the bottom of the street and would come in at least once a month to moan about the delivery truck waking her up early in the morning when they would drop off produce. Mrs Hollis Jr had moved in to the family estate at the end of the street, when she had married her husband, and had an air of grandeur about herself that would intimidate most people. However, Briar having grown up with her mother the way she was, so she was not scared of Mrs Hollis Jr. and was more than happy to comment if there was something that she didn't agree with. The party was a great money-maker and she could use the extra cash to add to her emergency fund, in case something broke in the shop. She also really liked providing the cakes for the party as it allowed her to show off her skills. With the success of the cheesecakes this morning, she thought she would spend a good twenty minutes, before her morning rush, to dust a couple of sugar flowers. Briar had an oversized baking tray that she kept all her sugar flower materials on. She liked to keep it all together, so that she could put it down whenever she needed to do another job.

The smell of bacon had taken over the desiccated coconut that usually hung in the air of the kitchen. She had already cut up the bread rolls and put the bacon under the grill ready for her 'morning boys', as she called them. Eight lads every morning, Monday to Saturday, would arrive at her shop at 7am on the dot to get a bacon roll and a cup of strong coffee.

The filter coffee pot beeped to show that it was full, as the knock on the door brought Briar out of her thoughts and back to reality. The time on the clock was 7.02am. She popped down her paintbrush that sent a small cloud of glitter dust in to the air, and, as she went to the front door, she flashed a quick smile at the men that were waiting outside the shop.

"Good morning" Briar greeted the boys, as she opened the door, and then turned back, to walk to the counter to begin serving.

"Your'right" said the first man through the door. He had a rough, Midland accent and the question of 'your'right' wasn't a question, it was just his way of saying good morning. His name was Philip and was the boss of the workmen crew, who were always Briar's first set of customers in the morning.

They had come to be some of Briar's regulars, after they had helped her chase a man who had stolen the charity box out of her shop window. Briar had chased him for a good half a mile, before she had run past the works crew, who had then tackled him to the ground and frog marched him to the police station. As a thank you, Briar had offered them a free bacon roll and a cup of coffee. The next morning, when she had opened the shop, they were waiting at the door and for the last eight months, they had turned it in to part of her morning routine.

Briar liked seeing them every morning and did a special breakfast rate for the boys. £3 for a bacon roll and a cup of coffee. Some of the lads had also started popping in with their families on the weekend, and having more customers was not a bad thing. This was made even more evident with the fact that a national coffee chain, called The Big Drip, had just moved in to a vacant shop, down the other end of the high road and with the fact that they could subsidise their coffee and cakes, any new customers were always welcome.

Briar got behind the counter, before she heard a laugh from a couple of the lads at the front of the queue.

"Well, you guys are certainly merry for a Monday morning," Briar quipped as she grabbed the tray of bacon from under the grill, using her monster hand oven mitt. She placed the tray on the counter, between the kitchen and the front counter, and went around to serve Philip.

"Shaun had a bachelor party this weekend," Philip explained, as she handed over a cup of black coffee and a bacon roll wrapped in a serviette. She scooped up the £3 in change that was on the counter, and dumped it in the till without counting it. Briar liked the fact that she could trust the boys to not short-change her.

"Ok," Briar acknowledged, "so did he have fun then?", As the next guy in the line moved forward. Briar repeated the motions handing him a bacon roll and cup of black coffee. He smiled as he gave her a £5. She popped the till and gave him his change.

"Oh yes," replied one of the other lads in the team, the guy with a split lip and the backwards baseball cap. Briar repeated the same motion of serving three more of the lads before she got to the man who had made that comment. Usually, Briar was polite, but tried no to engage in lots of conversation. This kept the line moving and allowed her to get more things done. But today the curiosity got the better of her and she asked, "Why?".

"He fell asleep and got a tattoo on his head" he replied with a big smile, as he took the bacon roll off the counter.

"Of what" Briar asked, as she put the money in the till. She looked up to notice the small, fat workman was next in line.

"His ex-girlfriend's name," he replied, as he bit in to the warm bacon roll and moved aside for the fat guy to get served.

"Can I….." the fat guy began to say before Briar cut him off mid-sentence.

"Brown roll, and a cup of decaf tea," she said with a smile, as she held out a hand for the £3, his order already waiting for him on the counter.

He smiled, and said thanks before moving off to the side to cover the bacon roll in red sauce. Briar always wanted to tell him that the amount of sugar and fat that went in to red sauce was not good for him, but, as she had reasoned with herself, he was a grown man and can make his own choices.

"No, Francesca went mad," the baseball cap guy replied, before throwing the empty napkin over the counter and in to the bin.

Briar smiled at his skills, before looking at the guys and counting. There were only seven of them this morning. "Shaun had to stay off work today…. got to get the tattoo removed from his head before the wedding next week," as he eyed up the unclaimed bacon roll. Briar knew that the food would just go to waste, so she handed it over to him and touched her fingers to her lips, indicating for the baseball-capped guy to not let on that she was giving away free food. He took the food and mouthed a thank you, before demolishing the second warm roll in three bites.

Briar put the unused coffee cup back on the stack and wiped the counter. She heard a couple of thankyou's and a good bye, before the boys left. Briar heard the front door close behind them, and she was again alone in her shop. She looked up to notice the guy with the baseball cap and the split lip smile at her. She smiled back and mindlessly touched her head, running her hand through her hair, before he headed off to join the rest of the boys, walking down the high road to work. After he had gone out of view, Briar let out a small nervous giggle. She was like any other girl, wanting to find someone to settle down with however, she had never had confidence and had always seen herself as the ugly duckling. She was happy to talk to anyone whom she didn't see as cute, but as soon as someone made their intentions known, she would start to get all defensive. Briar had openly admitted to friends that if there was a flirting course at the local college, she would be the first on the list.

She checked the temperature on the grill and walked over to the fridge to get out some more bacon and eggs. School and college kids would soon be coming through the front door and the need to plan for the morning rush was very important. To run a successful business, Briar couldn't afford to pay another full-time member of staff, so before the hordes of people came in the morning, she would get all the bread buttered, plates out and enough food cooked and being kept warm under the heat lamps to ensure that the line of customers kept moving.

There had been a group of girls in the shop yesterday afternoon to celebrate a baby shower and Briar had let one of them write on the chalk board, 'IT'S A BOY' in big letters. After getting out the three dozen eggs from the small pantry she wandered back round to the front with a wet cloth to clean off the announcement. The last thing she wanted was for one of her customers to assume that she was pregnant. Replacing the filter from the coffee pot she noticed that one of the lights on the front counter was out. Grabbing a pen from her apron she wrote lightbulb on the top of her left hand before swearing loudly. She had lent the step ladder to one of her neighbours, Mr Howard, who had never returned it and now that they no longer lived in the town, she would have no way of getting it back. One of the good things about the shop was the lovely high ceilings; however, the down side to that was if you stood on a table, you were still nowhere near reaching a bulb to replace it.

Pushing the blown bulb to the back of her mind, she continued to cook the breakfast. It was about twenty minutes before the front door opened again. Four school girls walked in dressed in, their green and black uniforms. Their skirts were not the shortest that Briar had ever seen, however they weren't far off. Their perfect hair and tiny ties indicated that they were part of the cool girl group. They strolled up to the counter and the head girl coughed.

"Just a moment," Briar yelled, as she took the first batch from the stove and put it under the heat lamp. "Hey, what can I get you?" she asked, getting got out a tray for the order.

"Can I have an egg roll please" She tossed a £10 on the counter. Briar took the money as she plated up the roll and handed the change.

"Coffee Please" said the next girl. Briar looked at her as she sighed a sweet smile with a head tilt.

"What year are you in?" asked Briar.

"Year nine," the girl replied, trying to maintain her eye contact.

"I am sorry, I'm not giving coffee to anyone under the age of fourteen."

"I am fifteen," said the girl, trying to keep the shakiness out of her voice.

"If you were fifteen, then you would be in year ten," remarked Briar in a nice even tone.

The teenager knew that she was busted and asked for a cup of tea without any more arguments. She handed over a £2 coin and moved away with the take away cup. The two girls behind her had heard the conversation and were ready for their argument.

"Two coffees please" said the taller of the girls and put £4 on the counter".

"As I said," began Briar, "not until you are fourteen. Tea?" as she got out two cups.

"We are in year ten, we would like our coffee please," said the shorter girl.

"No, you're not"

"Excuse me, are you calling me a liar?" asked the shorter girl.

"Yes" Briar in a very blunt way as she put her hands on her hips. If she could deal with Mrs Hollis Jr, she would not shy away from two children.

"I'm in year ten!" Both girls crossed their arms in front of them.

"If you are in year ten, then you would have been sorted in to your houses and have the colours sewn in to your blazers. As you haven't got a colour you are in year nine at the latest, so, you can have a cup of tea or a chocolate milk. Choose"

"How did you know about the houses" asked the shorter girl as she took her £2 off the counter.

"I went to Saint Michael's." Briar switched between addressing the shorter girl and the taller one. "Do you want a cup of tea?"

"Yes please," replied the taller girl as the short one went to go and join her class mates at the table, having been unsuccessful in extracting coffee from Briar.

Briar handed over the cup and said to her little customer, "I promise you that you will thank me in the long run. Caffeine stunts your growth."

"Like I need to be any taller" replied the girl with a smile. They left just as the next customer came in to the shop. Within twenty minutes, there was a long line of customers, who were quickly getting served. With an array of customers, the morning started to fly by. It was close to 10am before there was no one at the counter waiting to get served. Briar grabbed a big plate box and started to clear and wipe down all the empty tables after people had finished their breakfast. There was a copy of a novel, named 'Time Cottage', that had been left on the table. Briar flipped it over to read the number on the back, 23. That meant that it was a very old submission. Briar shoved it in to her apron and finished the clearing all in one go, not having to break the clean-up to go and serve anyone. She walked to the back of the counter to see one of her last customers standing their looking rather nervous. Briar walked past her and dumped the dirty dishes in front of the dishwasher before she came to see what her customer wanted. As she did, she managed to slam her left little toe in to the door frame that connected the door from the kitchen to the counter. She had to catch herself before she let out a massive swear word. She took in a deep breath and swallowed her pain before she spoke to the lady.

"Did you want anything else?" asked Briar, as she lobbed the novel through to the opening between the kitchen and front counter. It hit the middle counter and slid across the surface, before ending up on the floor in front of the fridge, picking up the now dry tea towel on the way through.

"Do you do take-away boxes?" asked the old lady as she browsed over the array of cakes and desserts, which were displayed over the front of the large counter.

She looked long and hard at a rather large chocolate sponge cake, before she looked up to find Briar resting her hip on the front counter.

"Yes, we do. Each cake is £2.40 a slice, but if you buy five slices I will do it for £10" Briar gingerly ran her stubbed foot up the back of her other leg, trying to assess if she had broken anything.

"No, I don't want a slice of cake. I want to buy a whole cake" Her eyes returned to the chocolate sponge.

Briar had never been asked for a cake from the display case before. She had made lots of cakes to order, having taken a request from Dr Holmes, the local GP, whose son was turning eighteen next week and she had ordered him a snooker table cake. But never one to turn down a sale, without skipping a beat, she had the cake boxed up and an extra £25 in the till in under thirty seconds. Briar usually liked to decorate the whole cakes that she sold a little more artistically, however having put her injured toe on the floor and the pain radiating up her whole foot, she decided to hand the cake over just as it was.

Briar hobbled around the shop for the rest of the morning, standing like a flamingo whenever the opportunity presented itself. Around midday, just before the lunchtime rush was about to start, Briar was running the last couple of dirty loads through the dishwasher and getting out sandwich filling from the fridge. Briar kicked the novel that she had thrown onto the counter and had ended on the floor. It was called 'Time Cottage', she propped it open on top of the recipe book, and after getting out the bread and a quick check to make sure that no one was waiting at the counter, she started to read the opening chapter.

The muddied, Red Land Rover rolled to a slow stop. ' Right, follow the plan, be nice' Mitchell remarked, as he pulled on the hand brake.

'Can you see the call button'? uttered Katie from the boot, as she curved her back in order to see past Sam and Leo, who were still asleep in the seats in front of her.

'Yes' shouted Mitchell back to his little sister who had been shoved in to the boot after a bad choice in rock, paper, scissors. She had chosen rock, over Sam's paper, and had regretted it for the last three hours; being squished in with the cases of beer and the two suitcases that Katie and Mona had packed, not to forget the big boxes at the bottom of the boot that contained a crucial element to their plan. The boys, wanting to pack light had each opted for a large rucksack. Mitchell's was in Mona's foot well and Katie had been sitting next to Sam and Leo's, one of which was giving off a strong smell of fish her money was on Leo's. 'I'll do it' exclaimed Mona, as she unclipped her seatbelt and opened the driver's side door. The sun had been blaring down on the south coast of England all of July and the 1st day of August was happily no different. Mona was appropriately dressed for the weather with her chequered red shirt, billowing open in the light breeze, over a black crop top tucked in to her daisy duke shorts, which her mother had renamed her hungry bum shorts. They always ended up being eaten by her bottom and she would have to keep removing them, but they were cool, comfortable and sexy, so she didn't mind the inconvenience of removing them when needed. Mona's boots made a crunch on the gravelled path, as she walked over to the call button. She read the black and red sign attached to front iron gate, that barred the path to Time Cottage -

'If you wish to gain access to Time Cottage, press the call button'

Mona walked up to the box and pressed her bright red polished thumb nail to the rusted silver box, which was catching the light, only on the button which was still shiny from repeated use, the rest of the box hand not been touched by anyone else for a long time. She waited 5 seconds and pressed it again.' What?' bellowed a rough voice from the metal box that had been slung over the rotting fence post on the side of the gravel road. Mona took a deep breath, remembering Mitchell's words to be nice ' Ah, hello', she said with a slight stutter, 'I would like to access Time Cottage please'. She started to consider if the person attached to the voice was male or female. 'Wait' it barked again 'my husband will be down to open the gate.' Mona gave a small smile as her own question had been answered. 'Thank you,' she said, but there was no response.

The sound of a chair being dragged across the bit of uncarpeted floor made Briar look out to the front of the shop. A mother, who had ordered a large coffee, had pivoted one of the lighter wooden chairs away from the windows and was currently breast feeding her infant.

Briar looked down at the mound of bread rolls that she had pre-made, and smiled to herself how many she had done without having to stop for a customer. She put the rest of the grated cheese in the bowl and moved on to the ham and tomato rolls. Briar liked the fact that she offered a small selection of sandwiches. She thought to herself that if people wanted the fennel and smoked salmon on sourdough, then they could go down to 'The Big Drip'. Her customers were happy with a nice crusty roll and a slice of homemade cake. Resting her hurt foot on the lower shelf, she returned to the novel. One of Briar's rules in the tea shop was that she would read all the books before she put them out for the public. But for the life of her she couldn't remember reading 'Time Cottage'. That meant one of two things, either she had read it and forgot about it, which meant that the writing was good but forgettable or that she had broken her own rule and put a book out without reading it. Briar was really enjoying the opening chapter and even though she knew that she had no hope of finishing the chapter before lunch rush started. She was interested to find out what happened next. So, she got out the ham and began to make up the next batch of rolls, while she continued to read.

Mona waited for a couple of seconds, but with the lack of reply, she turned tail and headed back to her dad's Land Rover'. He had lent it to Mitchell, in order for the five of them to complete the rescue mission, as they were calling it - the mission that had been cooked up a couple of weeks earlier by Mona, Mitchell and Sam.

Mona whispered, 'I called her, She said that he was gonna come and open the gates' as she got back in to the car, that was strewn with sweet wrappers and empty fast food cartons. 'I don't think that this is gonna be that easy' Mona was speaking in a delicate tone, as she didn't want to wake up Leo or Sam.

'It will be alright' said Mitchell at full volume, unaware of her intentions. As she leaned over and touched the inside of his thigh with her right hand, a small sexual gesture, but nothing that was too provocative, more of a self-protection measure, it was binding herself to her boyfriend in a physical and comforting way.

They sat in the car for a good five minutes, before the man appeared at the top of the lane. 'Heads up guys;' shouted Mitchell, as he swallowed the last boiled sweet from the silver tin that was resting on the dashboard and reflected ever so slightly in the windscreen. The noise from the driver's seat, woke up both Sam and Leo, who snorted awake in a little unplanned Abbott and Costello skit.

'Are we here?' asked Sam, as he gave a big yawn, but staring out of the window and recognising the familiar view, it confirmed that they had indeed reached their destination. Leo was rubbing his eyes, as if he had been awoken from a deep sleep.

'Yep,' said Mitchell 'and he doesn't look happy'. Mitchell took a deep breath as he got out of the Land Rover and proceeded to lean on the bonnet in a model like pose. His stripy blue shirt was tucked in to his blue faded jeans, a man that was effortlessly fashionable combined with his handsome frame and quick wit. Mona referred to him as a triple threat - an attractive body, great style and a mind to rival most Oxford graduates; Mona would catch herself occasionally staring at her boyfriend, whom she loved to death.

'Good morning, Sir,' Mitchell shouted to the old gentleman, who was opening the gate.

'One minute,' shouted the old man, as he swung the gate open. 'Drive in to the middle of the pen.'

With no other conversation offered, Mitchell got back in his Land Rover.

'Is he a complete bastard?' quipped Katie from the boot.

'Katie, shush,' stated Mitchell in a hushed tone. 'I think you're right. This is not gonna be easy.' Mitchell said to Mona, as he put the car in first gear, rolled through the first gate and stopped in the pen. The gentleman closed and padlocked the first gate before moving on to the second gate, which was also padlocked. He looked in no hurry to help the Land Rover get to Time Cottage.

He opened the second gate that allowed the car to be released from the iron pen. All five members of the car smiled and waved to the grumpy old man who stood holding open the second gate with the heel of his muddy shoe. He didn't acknowledge the people and their kind gestures, but started to close and lock the second iron gate.

Briar was so engrossed in reading whilst making the lunches, that she hadn't heard the front door jingle, or the bell on the front counter beep. "Excuse me, hello. Does anyone actually work in this establishment?" a posh, older male voice could be heard saying from the other side of the counter.

Briar quickly finished stuffing a ham roll as she called "Coming" from in the kitchen. She shoved the second tray full of rolls in reach of the serving hatch and hobbled round to find a small smartly dressed man, in a suit and tie, standing at the counter. His flat cap was hiding what Briar assumed to be an oversized head, that looked way too big for the rest of his body. She noticed the scars on his hands and smiled warmly at him, as she came to rest opposite him behind the glass display cabinet that had previously held the large chocolate cake. This Briar had forgotten to replace with one of her emergency fruit cakes from a tin in the back of the kitchen.

"What can I get you?" asked Briar as she re-assumed the flamingo position. She smiled again; however, this time it was not at the customer. She was remembering how bad she was at gymnastics so that standing on one leg was almost impossible. If only she had known that injury made her well balanced.

"I would like a cup of tea and a cup of coffee," stated the gentleman, without taking a breath, as if he had inhaled and was waiting for a question to be asked, so he could start breathing again.

"Sure, what kind of tea would you like?", as she motioned the array of different tea boxes that sat on the thin, wooden shelves behind her.

"Normal breakfast tea, and the coffee to be filtered."

Briar felt the coffee pot, it was still piping hot and she poured it with her left hand as she leant across to the English breakfast tea pot and made up the order. "Any cakes or sandwiches to go with the drinks?" She put them on a tray and pushed the tray towards the gentleman.

"You could throw in a couple of scones with jam," he replied as he gestured over the £5 note that he was holding. Briar got the scones from the display cabinet and placed them on the tray with a knife. She noticed the money and went to the till to ring up the order, "That will be £7.20 please" She leant down to get the array of jams that she kept cool under the front counter.

"The scones should be free, as I had to wait to get served," said the gentleman, as if he had asked for a napkin.

Briar stopped reaching for the jam and looked at her customer in disbelief. In the time since she had taken over the shop, she had not been seriously asked to hand over free food. "Look, I am sorry that you had to wait a couple of seconds, but you are not having the scones for free" Briar looked the gentleman dead in the eye with one hand on the tray of items. He opened his wallet and retrieved another crisp £5 note. As he handed it over to Briar, he remarked, "You should sharpen up a bit on your service."

Briar knew how word of mouth could affect a business, but, with the fact that her foot really hurt and that she was starting to feel how little sleep she had actually had the night before, she retaliated, "I run a successful business on my own, and you had to wait ten seconds to get served. I am sharp enough" She plucked the money from his hand. "Raspberry or Strawberry jam?" She retorted as she put the change on the tray.

Briar didn't know if the gentleman was shocked that he had been addressed with the same amount of disdain that he had given over the counter, but he mumbled "Strawberry please" as she leant back down to get the jam. Briar, however, hadn't finished him off to her satisfaction and upon placing two sets of jam sachets on the tray, she leant forward and said, "And its rude to wear your hat inside," before purposefully stepping to her left so that she could begin to serve the next customer.

As she got the following lunch order ready she watched him hobble over to the old lady with his tail between his legs. The enjoyment that Briar had felt dressing him down evaporated and she started to feel sorry for him. He was rude and there was no denying that, but Briar knew that she didn't know what was going on in his life and she could have easily taken the high road. She had not given him free food, but there was no need to speak to him the way that she had done. She wrapped up the large lunch order in a brown bag, took payment and then reached back under the counter for a couple more packets of jam. As she hobbled round, she hit the floorboard and felt her heart jump slightly out of her chest. When she got over to the old couple, she waited for them to look up before she started speaking.

"You don't get a lot of jam in those sachets, so I thought I would bring over a couple more" She said as she placed the jam on to the table between them. "Just let me know if you need any more milk" she added, before heading back to the counter and tackling the long list of customers that had begun to arrive. As she hobbled back, her foot still hurt, but her body felt a lot lighter. Briar wasn't someone who was all superstitious or religious; however, she did believe in karma. Being nice to the old couple, somehow, had put her back on balance and she knew that she would feel better for the rest of the day. Briar had always had a very long memory in terms of regret. She knew that it would have niggled away at her, got under her skin. And once they had left the shop, she wouldn't have been able to change the way she had left the conversation.

The rest of the lunch rush whizzed by; Carole the florist from across the road, came in for her usual afternoon fruitcake. So, Briar traded a free cup of coffee for a chance to whiz upstairs and use the bathroom. Carol liked the deal. Being a coffee fanatic and filling her large soup bowl full of the good coffee, not the filtered one, in exchange for allowing someone to wee without having to shut her shop up, was a really good deal.

Briar rubbed in the moisturising cream in to the back of her hand as she walked down the stairs back to the shop. She could have used the customer bathroom, but she liked the fact that she could wee in peace. And by peace she meant that she could check her social media account as the Wi-Fi for the flat wasn't strong enough to reach downstairs. She had posted about the cheesecakes, that she had baked that morning, and the post had received thirty-seven likes. There had also been a comment asking where the shop was and most of Briar's decompression time had been spent trying to attach a copy of direction to the reply post. She thanked Carole and allowed her to leave with her vat of coffee, wondering how many times she had been able to fill it up in the time she had been upstairs. Briar knew better than to comment on the extra coffee theft and she was sure she got more out of the deal, with Carole. Whom, was always dropping off the cut offs from flower orders that she could put in the window for a couple of days. Once, a wedding had been called off the day before the ceremony and Carole had walked over with lots of foxgloves that she put in the window for free; the trade of an extra couple of pounds of coffee a month wasn't so bad.

The day trundled on as normal. The new postman popped in around five and commented on the fact that she had another three packages to take delivery of. The evening mother and baby class, that was usually held at the local community centre, had been cancelled and the three toddlers who had just sat down with their mums, were not taking the 'no soft play today' news well. The new postman was lovely and Briar was sure, once she had explained that he wasn't delivering lots of catalogues, but novel submissions for the shop, the comments would change dramatically. She contemplated bringing it up as she took the packages from him, but with the decibel level of the shop being rather high from the screaming toddlers, she thought better of it.

CHAPTER 3

By the end of the day, Briar was sitting alone in her living room, staring again at the chapter on Helen's death, with a bowl of homemade chilli cooling beside her. She had managed to shut the shop for thirty minutes that afternoon and browse over the three CVs that she had decided to interview the next day regarding the Saturday job. During a particularly slow twenty minute window, she had made two batches of cheese scones that were still cooling on the wire racks in the shops kitchen downstairs. It was 8.30pm and the long writing session from the night before was starting to show on her face, her feet felt all tingly, stretched out under the coffee table. She dragged herself off the floor, her right knee cracking as she stood up and wandered in to the bathroom. She had one small egg-shaped bath bomb left that she dropped from waist height. The water hadn't got to the other end of the bath yet and it smashed open on the old cast iron tub. Reaching around the doorframe to her makeup table, Briar grabbed the top package that had been dropped off by the postman. As she unwrapped the submission a load of gold and purple sparkles spilled out of the package and onto Briar's large, black bath mat. Briar swore loudly and the whole novel slipped out of the packaging and onto her injured foot. She let out a small yelp and then began to curse the person who had sent in the submission. "What kind of an idiot does that?" as she looked down at her feet to see her left one turning an even darker shade of red, the stars glittered against the bathroom light and sprinkled on to the bath mat, making it look like an attempt to create a night's sky. Briar lent back on to the bath and turned off the taps. The egg bath bomb had stopped dissolving and had turned the water a beautiful shade of orange. She quickly took off her clothes, leaving the mess on the bathroom floor and slowly lower herself into the steaming hot bath and let out a sigh of relief once she had submerged her shoulders under the water. She lifted her feet above the water line to compare them, but with the water being so hot, they both looked a nice, rosy pink. She lay there for about twenty minutes letting her muscles relax, and breathing in the scent of jasmine.

Running her hand through the water the colour made her think of the roses that were in her kitchen downstairs. The blood orange one from Jack would have to go the next day, Briar really didn't want to throw it out. The last thing she did, before heading back up the stairs, was to put out the empty milk bottle and leave the loose tea leaves ready for the pick-up in the morning. As normal, when upstairs, Briar was wearing a high bun and she tried to remember how greasy her hair was when she had looked in the mirror earlier. She couldn't remember thinking that it looked that bad and hoped that it could stretch another day before it needed a wash. This Thursday was Jack's drop-in day to collect the milk money and Briar always made a special effort to look nice. So not washing her hair that night would fit in very well with her plans and also her energy levels. Using her right foot to turn the tap she added some more water to the bath and then dried her hands on the big towel, before scooping up the novel that she had left on the floor. She shook it to make sure that there were no more sparkly things in between the pages and looked at the title. 'Impact'. She turned the first page and was met with...

A Warning

.....in big letters at the top of the page. Briar contemplated lobbing it back over the bath and worrying it about it the next day, but she reasoned with herself that if she read the first couple of chapters, she would be able to tell if it was ok to put downstairs. Briar had a regular customer, that she had named Purple Beret Lady, who came in everyday and when she ordered her tea and cake she always asked if there was anything new in. Briar thought that it would be nice if she could present her with a brand-new novel that would tide her over for a few days. It would put a smile on her face and would make her stay a bit longer than normal. Briar had barely admitted it to herself, but The Big Drip was going to steal some of her customers and the more inviting she could make her shop, the better. So, she cracked her neck, turned off the hot water and began to read.

If you are reading this in a public place, I will ask you a question. How much attention have you paid to the people around you? Did you make a snap judgement or decision about them? Now imagine going through the worst event of your life and all you have is the people around you right now. With a traumatic event comes knowledge of strangers. The names of the dead and injured will be on public record – your families will know more about the people that you are around than you will. They will know their ages, occupations, marital status and now, with the way that the world is going, the religious status of all the people affected. The people you meet, and the people you see, are all set on a journey. This is not a journey of self-discovery, but the E9 Coach that is departing from Victoria Coach station at 11o'clock, with its scheduled destination of Lincoln at 5 o'clock. The two stops in between are Nottingham Bus Station and Stoke-on-Trent Bus Station. This coach will depart on time; however, it will sadly not arrive in Nottingham. On the M1, there will be an accident. All the passenger's will be injured. There will be blood and death.

Oh Crikey, thought Briar, closing her eyes for a second as a bit of undissolved bath bomb was lodged by her leg and began to tickle the back of her knee as it fizzed.

 As a society, people are aware of mortality, however, do not wish to dwell on it. When pressured, they say, 'I want to die in my own bed, surrounded by family' or 'go in my sleep, that would be nice'. The people you know, see regularly on the tube, live next door to and are about to meet, fall in to this demographic. However, there is a ray of sunshine. One person will hear the voice of the emergency services, open their eyes and eventually walk away from the crash. One person will feel relief from pain, and indeed fall into a deep sleep, and poetically die with a family member holding their hand. How the strange choice of one person can affect the lives of so many and the mundane decision of where to sit can dictate the rest of your life.

Briar took a deep breath and re-read the writing. It was formatted in that stupid Gothic text and she found that rather distracting. She guessed that the writer was a woman, probably slightly older than her, late thirties and with a need for a new challenge. Briar knew that she would probably never find out who sent in their submissions, but she was very happy that she had decided to sit in the bath and start reading. The water now was getting cold and she flexed her foot to check to see how it was feeling. It had stopped hurting so she popped the novel on the toilet seat lid and stood up in the bath.

Briar hopped out and wrapped herself in the towel, leaving the book where it was. She wandered back in to the living room and grabbed the chilli bowl that had now gone cold. She stood scrunching up her toes in the carpet, as she shovelled the chilli into her mouth. She liked the feeling of the shag carpet on her toes and thought back to when she had seen it in a film. It was supposed to be good for de-stressing, but Briar mainly liked the sensation it gave her feet. After finishing the chili, she wandered into the kitchen and flicked the kettle on. She rubbed herself dry and hung the towel on the back of the kitchen door. Standing there, naked, in the kitchen, she selected a mug from the shelf and tossed in a decaf nettle tea bag. She grabbed the half-full bottle of whiskey from behind the sink and added a healthy two fingers to the mug before replacing the cap. Adding the hot water, she could smell the single malt. Allowing the tea to mash for a couple of seconds, she threw the spoon into the sink, along with the teabag.

Leaving the kitchen, she stopped in the hallway, trying to make up her mind between going to the bedroom and allowing herself at least seven hours of sleep or to reassume the position in front of her laptop to decide what to do with her 'Helen Problem' as she had dubbed it to herself.

Placing the mug on the bedside table she pulled on her bed clothes and wandered into the living room to shut her laptop down and turn off all the lights, apart from the one on her bedside table. Snuggling under the covers, she enjoyed the cold sheets on her skin. She drank the tea in three large gulps and flicked the light off. It was 10pm and Briar couldn't remember the last time she had been in bed before midnight. She fell asleep with her hands resting on her boobs. The kettle flicked off, Cleo jumped on to the chair at the end of Briar's bed and both of them were snoring before the alarm clock read 10.03pm.

Briar opened the front door to the shop. As she had a limited amount of time to do the interview, she was going to see them all together. Three frozen people stood before her. A middle-aged lady with a plump smile and a bonny hat greeted her first. "Thank you so much for this interview", she said, in a slightly patronising voice.

Briar smiled and introduced herself with an outstretched arm.

"Briar Carter, nice to meet you." She went straight from the plump lady to the middle-aged gentleman "Hello," she said with a smile.

"Michaels, M. Pleasure," he replied in a curt, open tone. He was a Scotsman. And judging by his hair cut and his shiny boots he was almost certainly ex-military. He wore well fitted suit trousers and a shirt buttoned up to the collar, but no tie. Resembling an Essex boy look without the attitude or trainers.

Taken aback slightly by his strong hand shake, Briar moved on to the third member of the party.

"Hi" Briar offered, as to the other interviewee, her hand, He was wearing a new white shirt that had just been freshly ironed and was slightly too big for him. He looked completely uncomfortable and as out of place. He took her hand and smiled weakly, not saying anything in reply. On his right thumb, he had two tattoos - a small owl and '71. Briar also noticed that in his free hand he had a couple of books; a book of poetry and 'The Great Tragedy' by Susan Carnell. Briar recognised the front cover, as the book had lived on her desk for the last year of university. Whilst studying classics at uni, the Shakespearean reference book had become very useful in answering essay questions.

"You like reading then," she said to the lad, as he stepped in to the shop. He adjusted the grip on the books, but didn't reply.

Briar took charge with, "Would you all like to sit down? – I have put a pot of tea on," as she gestured to the prepared table next to the fireplace. "Thank you all for coming," she continued happily. The plump lady had the big arm chair and took off her coat. A waft of perfume filled the area. It was a sweet musky smell. …Briar slightly inhaled and proceeded to quell a cough immediately. The smell reminded her of an old next-door neighbour and although she had only happy memories of the old lady, she had a knot appear in her stomach that filled her with a brief feeling of dread. She shook it off and asked, "Anyone for tea?" as she leant forward and picked up the big tea pot.

"Oh, yes please that would be lovely," remarked the plump lady, as she shuffled and picked up a cup ready.

"No thank you," replied Mr Michaels, J.

The younger lad uttered his first word to Briar – "Please".

Once the tea had been handed out, Briar's brain was working overtime. She had spent the morning thinking of things to ask them, while she iced Mr Lambert's anniversary cake; however, for the life of her, she could not remember anything that she had planned to ask.

"Do you live local?" she aimed the question directly to the young lad who she was aware from his application, was called Carl and had 'decided' to take a year out before heading off to university. He was off to Leeds to read classics with film studies and Briar understood that there was a desire to get out of the monotonous town and to see the world. Before he could even open his mouth to reply, Briar heard the plump lady, who was called Rebecca, answer.

"Well, I live in the lovely village of Mead, just over the hill." In a bright tone, she followed it up with, "So, I'm always on hand if you need me for anything last minute".

Briar acknowledged Rebecca with a head nod and a brief smile, before returning her attention to Carl.

"And what about you?", looking directly in to Carl's eyes. To Briar's surprise, at how timid he had been from the start of the meeting, he looked directly at her. His dull grey eyes had a yellow tinge around the edges and there was sleep in his left eye, that was just hanging off some eyelashes. 'I live down the road" he replied with a gesture to the end of the high road.

"Nice and close then. I can't remember you popping in the shop though? Have you been here before?" Briar took a slight pause and then added the word "Carl?" as she didn't want Rebecca to start talking and disrupt the flow of the conversation that was building. She hadn't looked over, but she suspected that she had taken a deep breath to start talking and had probably stopped herself when she said Carl.

"Yeah, a couple of times. I like Cleo. She comes and sits on my lap, when I order a sandwich," Carl said, maintaining eye contact. Briar was starting to get a bit self-conscious and shuffled in her seat awkwardly.

"By any chance, do you get a tuna sandwich – any cat will make friends with anyone for tuna," Rebecca said with a slight giggle. The condescending tone was even more evident.

"You've met Cleo?" Briar acknowledged "She is her own boss, that's for sure".

"Speak to me….what is it, home, mince not to the general tongue?" Carl said. Mr Michaels had turned his face for the first time to look at Carl. Rebecca had stopped giggling and now looked worried, as if she had allowed herself to be in the same vicinity as a lunatic.

"Yes, Yes," Briar exclaimed as she put down her tea cup and brought her foot up to sit under her bum. "Name Cleopatra, as she is called in Rome".

"We read it for A-level" Carl offered as an explanation, before he lowered his head and became very interested in the nail of his index finger.

"It's my favourite Shakespeare," Briar replied, looking round the shop for Cleo. She couldn't see her and turned her attention to the only candidate that she hadn't spoken to.

Briar looked at Mr Michaels, who seemed to be viewing her in a non- direct but constant manner, as if ready to react to any scenario.

"And Mr Michaels" she began in a friendly manner, "do you have a first name? I like to have quite an informal relationship with anyone that I work with" Briar stopped fidgeting and looked at him, "It wasn't on the application form."

He looked at her, as if he was trying to sum her up. Briar felt she was being assessed for worth. He cleared his throat and coughed a couple of times.

"Marion", he answered with a dead pan expression, not looking at either of the people who were effectively competing for the job with him.

"Hi" Briar responded. She didn't laugh at the unusual name. She felt better now. The tension in the air began to lift and she took a big gulp of her tea, before refilling her cup. "And what part of Scotland are you from?". Being keen to keep the ball rolling, she had a good vibe from him and didn't want to say the wrong thing. She didn't think that if she had been guessing for a week she would have thought he looked like a Marion. But in an odd way it suited him. A strange fact popped in to her head that John Wayne's first name was Marion and he instantly looked like he had a British cowboy vibe - not getting stressed. Happy in silence and able to control a conversation. The kind of man that was very secure in his personality.

Marion looked at her, as if there was a smile hidden in his cheek "Now you have either got a very good ear or have been very lucky" not in a mean tone, but with an air of knowing.

"Why?" Briar asked with a slight amount of apprehension. Still thinking about the unusual name choice, she was now worrying as to where she had gone wrong.

"I was born in Scotland, but raised in Cardiff," he continued, "and I have been told by my sister that I now have a Welsh accent not a Scottish one". Briar began to question herself on her deduction of accents. Did the man sound

Welsh? Living in such a boring little town as this, everyone spoke the same - southern, posh with a slight underlay of over pronouncing the words to keep up with everyone else. Briar called it the keeping up appearances accent. Briar had lived all her life in Sussex and was convinced that when people got drunk and started slipping their 'N's and 'H's, they talked how they should really do all the time. Rebecca had gone slightly pink and looked like she was trying to hold in a giggle, but didn't dare to show it, as she looked unsure as to how Marion would take her laughing at his name. He looked like a man, who could dress you down with just a few short words. Briar had discovered, from his application form, that he had served in the armed forces and had retired 5 years earlier. She was imagining British intelligence, with the fate of the country coming down to a man called Marion who now wanted a job in Briar's tea shop.

"Why would you want a job here?" she asked.

Rebecca seized upon the undirected question and jumped in, "I think this place has so much character and its definitely full of…. my kind of people. I believe that I would bring an air of comfort and happiness to the café". She took a deep breath, before adding, "not that it isn't homely now. I can just see myself fitting in very well" and with that statement, she shuffled her plump little bottom on the chair and crossed her ankles out in front of her, just as if she was sitting in her living room at home.

"Thank you," Briar replied, a little wobble evident in her voice. "Homely, is what I go for" and as she turned her head thinking about the comment, "my kind of people". Briar thought about her clients and which ones were Rebecca's kind of people. She was sure not Rebecca meant her 'Morning Boys'.

Rebecca added, "I am also a very good cook. I can make all kinds of dishes so I would be useful in the kitchen as well as managing the customers out here". The hairs on the back of Briar's neck stood up at the word 'manage'. She thought to herself that if she gave Rebecca the job, within six months she would be wanting to change the menu and run the kitchen.

That was the second Briar decided Rebecca would not be getting the job and it would be a miracle for her to be asked any other questions. Physically turning her whole body away from Rebecca and towards Carl, she asked the same question. Carl had been crumbling a sugar cube in to his tea. In doing so he had managed to get most of it on his trousers. Seeming to be oblivious to the mess that he was making, he continued to crumble, as he answered Briar's question.

"My mum said that I needed a job," he replied. Briar was not enthused by the fact that the reason he was sitting in front of her was because his mother had wished it. Then he added, "and I like cake," before attempting to pick up another sugar cube from the bowl with his fingers, having just licked off the residual sugar from the last crumble. Briar, however, got there first and picked up the sugar bowl. Trying to play the movement off as natural, she put a sugar cube in her own tea, something that she never did, as she found that Elderflower and Acia tea is at its best when it was on its own without any sweeteners. She then placed the sugar bowl on a side table, well out of arms reach of Carl and his crumbly fingers. This interview was not going that well for Briar. To her right, she had a lady who obviously thought a lot about herself, and to her left, a boy, who was mainly there out of his mother's insistence; Briar was quite sure he saw it to make some money and eat as much free cake as possible while doing it. Briar thought Carl seemed smart, but the flippant answers and the non-connected way of talking, sealed the deal for a definitive, "NO".

Briar looked at Marion and tried to not reveal that she thought he was her last hope. She looked straight at the man who was sitting opposite her. He was sitting up straight, his hands resting on his knees, Marion was waiting his turn and was aware that it was now his chance to speak, but he didn't jump the gun and start talking. He waited for Briar to ask, "Why do you want to work here?".

Marion didn't answer straight away. He cleared his throat again and asked in a sincere way "Why would I not want to? The company has always been pleasant, when I have ventured inside. It is efficiently run. The breakdown of my duties has all been outlined well. I think it would be a very nice place to put down some roots." Briar's face represented a cod fish. She had the same hairs sticking up on her neck, but this time it was for a good reason - she was getting excited. Briar thought to herself that the answer was so well crafted that it must have been prepared beforehand. However, it was delivered in such an off the cuff way, and so genuine that if she had asked him to repeat himself, then she wasn't sure that he could do it. Rebecca sunk a little in her chair. The atmosphere of the room had changed and Briar had the biggest grin on her face. She could even feel it in her ears, the smile was that wide.

She knew that she couldn't just ask one question, but Mrs Hollis Jr's cakes were in the oven and if they were even one minute overdone, she wouldn't be able to use them. She quickly asked, "Do you live close, Marion," making a conscious effort to not look at her watch again.

"I will do, soon," he replied and without any elaboration Briar decided to end the interviews there.

Briar checked her watch, but didn't look at the time. "Right, thank you all for coming," she said as she stood up and moved towards the door. Rebecca and Carl followed suit. Rebecca was at the door first. She waited for Briar to undo the lock, before she shook Briar's right hand with both of hers.

Saying "Thank you, thank you so much" as she did so, Briar got another large waft of her perfume and tried not to cough.

Briar thought that if Rebecca hadn't shaken her hand so obviously then Carl would have just said bye. But he did shake hers and when they connected, she could feel the sugar grains that were in between their two palms. Briar felt instantly sick; the idea of grainy sugar made her stomach flip up. She thought that it felt unnatural and weird and the idea that she was going to have to now shake Marion's hand. Briar watched Carl walk up the High Road and noticed Mrs Hollis Jr. standing outside the barber's. Briar guessed that she was waiting for her husband; however, not wanting to be seen by Mrs Hollis Jr, she ducked her head back in the shop quickly. After the recoil from Carl's sugar hand, she had been frantically, and equally subtly, trying to scrape the residue of sugar off her hand before she would shake Marion's. However, by the time that she turned and expected to see Marion standing there, waiting to say his goodbyes, she found him in the midst of standing up. This gave her enough time to give her hand a good wipe on her bottom. She looked round at him and as he approached, he kept his hands behind his back. To

Briar, he looked even taller than he had done when he had first sat down. His head would have easily grazed the door frame to the cupboard, under the stairs, where she kept the cleaning supplies. Once Marion had said his goodbye's and began walking up the road, Briar heard the rustle of papers. It was the CV's that Briar had left on her chair after the interview. She gathered them up and popped them next to the flower vase, on top of the old fridge. The Rose that Briar had got that morning was standing to attention. It was a deep crimson colour and looked beautiful, with a small amount of dew still attached to the petals. When she got in to the kitchen she glanced at the clock on the wall. She had five minutes before she had scheduled to re-open the shop, which meant that she had just enough time to wee and clear away the tea set left out from the interview. As she walked round the table to the connecting door to the flat, she noticed the pint of milk had the letter V on it. She thought for a couple of seconds what the V meant. It was Tuesday and she briefly thought about asking Jack, when she would see him on Thursday what the letters meant. Briar had asked her friend Carol if she had anything written on her milk bottles. Carol had answered the question with a categorical, "No".

As she ascended the stairs to her flat, she smiled at the decision that she had made to hire Marion and thought that she would ring all three of them the next day and tell them the verdict. Briar's thoughts snapped back to the milk bottles. Today it was a V and yesterday it was an O. After Briar finished in the bathroom, she remembered that she had three cakes in the oven and ran down the stairs very quickly. She managed to get the cakes out of the oven before they went too brown. Briar had planned for them to be naked cakes, decorated with flowers and fruit, but they were dark enough to invite a response from Mrs Hollis Jr, or one of her cronies so, Briar grabbed the big mixer from under the central counter and got to work, making butter cream icing.

Jack had just finished his morning rounds and was taking the long way back to the depot. The hum of his electric engine was very soothing to him, and, as he couldn't pick up his dry cleaning until after 9am, he had some time to kill.

He reached the top of the high road and stopped when he noticed the blue rose that he had left that morning discarded on the pavement. He looked from the rose to the front of the shop. The door was open and he could see one of the lightweight wooden chairs on its side. He drove the cart down to stop in front of the shop. Searching the bay windows for any clue as to what had happened in the forty minutes since he had delicately placed the rose for Briar next to the milk.

Jack instinctively reached in to his pocket; he felt the loose tea packet with the gold bows before turning off the engine and getting out of the cart. Being at least a head taller than the cart, he didn't look like he could comfortably sit in there, but Jack always said that it was the comfiest thing he had ever driven. He saw Cleo's tail curl around the dustbins and out of sight and realised that his heart was pumping fast inside his chest.

There was a clatter of something and then the sound of running water could be heard from the kitchen "Oh bugger. Oh bugger!" Jack heard Briars voice echo through the empty shop. Looking through the open door, he could see a shattered bottle of milk that was strewn across the front steps.

He felt a lump rise in this throat, when he noticed a couple of spots of blood splattered in with the milk. With a quick leap, he tried to jump over the milk and glass but underestimated it and landed on his bum in a pile of milk, knocking in to a table with a loud clatter, as he hit the floor. Jack sat there in the milk for a moment, stunned, then he heard the water turn off and a pair of slow footsteps got louder and louder. Jack, who had ended up sitting, facing the door, cautiously turned his head and instantly recognised Briars purple shoes standing next to him. Their eyes met before either of them spoke. Her face was flushed and wet from crying. She was holding her left hand which was wrapped in a white tea towel that had been splattered with blood. Jack suspected if you laid out the tea towel, it would resemble a Jackson Pollock piece.

"Hi," Jack said in a sheepish tone. As he got himself to his feet, he could feel the cold milk seeping through his jeans and down his leg.

"Hi, yourself," replied Briar, still cradling her hand. She twisted her wrist slightly and winced at the pain.

"Oh lord!" exclaimed Jack, trying to retain some dignity. "Sit down" he said, as he pulled out the chair that he had crashed in to, "I'll get the mop".

Briar looked at Jack and then to the chair, being asked to take a seat in her own tea shop was a first. "Thanks," she said. Briar just sat there with her hand slowly oozing blood, and watched Jack, whose pale blue jeans had started to dry stiff from where he had landed in the milk. He shut the shop door and swept up as much glass as possible. With the strategic placement of the carpets, half of the disaster zone was being absorbed by the fabric and Briar's thoughts briefly turned to online videos of how to get milk out of an old carpet, without spending too much money.

Briar hadn't seen him venture outside, but he must have done, as the lights on his cart had been turned off and that day's blue rose, was now resting on one of the velvet armchairs, on the opposite side of the shop. He disappeared in to the kitchen. As Briar started to examine his handy work, she had been so focused on her hand that she had barely looked at Jack, working around her. The milk had been cleared and there was no trace of glass anywhere. She had sat in silence while he worked, feeling embarrassed at the accident. He then came back in to view, with a tea towel over his shoulder, carrying a cup of tea and a medical box.

"I found this under the sink," he said, presenting the medical box. He moved the chair opposite Briar and sat down, so that his right knee slotted in between Briar's legs. The two were not touching, but it made a small knot appear in Briar's stomach and she realised the proximity of him to her.

"I don't think that that will work," remarked Briar, indicating the med box with her head, as she picked up the tea cup with the non-injured hand and tried to smell the type. It was a normal tea bag and she was guessing that he had taken it out one of the boxes randomly and been lucky it was one to which you were supposed to add milk.

"I was in the army. They gave us all first aid training" Jack assured Briar, laying the first aid box on the table and subsequently opening it.

Briar didn't know what to say. She could lie and say, 'Oh really. Were you in the armed forces? I had no idea'. Or she could confess the truth and admit that she had spent a larger than healthy amount of time online, learning all about his life, specifically his relationship status. Not knowing what to say, she just smiled and pushed her injured arm slightly towards Jack.

"Plus, I did a first aid course at the church when I was eighteen. It will be fine," Jack added.

Briar stifled a laugh, as she placed the tea cup back on the mismatched saucer. "What?" Jack asked cautiously, taking his first good look at the injury.

"That's not a medical kit,' she answered.

Jack flipped open the lid and saw the kit was filled to the brim with sea shells.

"Ok," he replied in complete astonishment.

"They're from a long time ago. Actually, I'd forgotten about them."

"Well, we should probably see the damage". As he moved his hands towards Briars wrist, she instinctively pulled away from him slightly.

"I won't hurt you. I promise," he assured her and Jack noticed that her whole arm relaxed slightly and he pulled her wrist slightly toward him. He unwrapped the napkin, as if he was performing major surgery. The cut was not too deep. Jack rolled up Briar's sleeve, from the wrist to the elbow, being very careful to not snag the button on the open wound.

That is when he saw it, a burn mark in the shape of a rose, Imprinted at the top of her forearm. It looked sore around the outside and had a slight amount of scarring that wrapped round to the tip of her elbow. Jack tried to hide the fact that he had seen the scar, by focusing on the cut. The wound had stopped bleeding and the blood was beginning to clot. Briar tried to cover up the burn with her other hand, but she knew that it was too late. Jack now knew her secret. He didn't know the meaning behind the scar, but she couldn't hide it from him anymore. She wasn't ashamed of the scar, not in the traditional sense. Her Mother, Rose had placed a paper weight, in the design of a rose, on the stove and branded her with it, after a moaning session to her friend, about how much she hated working in the shop, had been overheard. And reported back to the disgust of her mother. It was child abuse, Briar knew that. What she was ashamed of was not the scar, but the fact that when she told the story to anyone, she would have to admit that she wasn't brave enough to speak up against what her mother had done, and worse, she hadn't been strong enough to defend herself against her mother.

"Have you got anything to dress it with?", Jack asked, obviously trying to retain the focus on the new injury and not drawing attention to Briar's embarrassment.

'No,' she replied meekly. As she shifted in the chair, her right knee came to rest on Jack's knee. Luckily, not the one that was now drying rigid from the milk spillage.

'OK then', He calmly re wrapped the wrist and said in a firm but sweet voice, "we're going to the hospital".

After Jack's remark about going to the hospital, neither of them had made a move to stand up. They just sat there, looking at each other, before Jack said

"Guess you're not too fond of the blue roses then. I will remember that for next time," with a smile.

"No, I really like them," said Briar, meeting his eyes.

Jack got to his feet and took Briar's good hand and helped her up, as if she was a pensioner. She let out a gasp of pain when the skin moved around the wound.

"Here, rest your arm across your chest like this," suggested Jack, moving her arm over her boobs.

"Thanks," said Briar, positioning herself closer to him.

Jack thought for a second about kissing Briar, but before he could act on it, she blurted out

"Shit, Oh Shit" and that killed the mood.

"What?" he asked, looking intently at her wrist to see if it was bleeding again or out of place.

"My morning boys" she replied as she strode back to the kitchen to put the bacon under the grill one handed. Briar flashed a glance at the clock; it read 6.55am.

Jack, whom had been hot on her heels appeared in the doorway to the kitchen before he asked, "Who are your morning Boys?" in a half concerned, half defensive tone.

"They are a group of lads that I serve bacon and coffee to every morning at 7am" She put the bacon under the grill and went to get the rolls from the bread bin.

"I think..." Jack began, before Briar cut him off midsentence.

"Could you put two scoops of coffee in the top of the filter please?" She grabbed the butter out of the fridge, suddenly very aware that the flowers Jack had left for her were in full view. As she looked over at him, she saw a hint of a smile leave his face, when he looked from above her head back to her and then focused on the task he had just been given.

"I'm sure that they won't mind missing one morning as you are injured," stated Jack, flicking the coffee filter on and walking round the front counter in to the doorway between the shop and the kitchen.

"I know they probably wouldn't, but they spend £500 a month in the shop, and I can't take that chance". She managed to pop the top off the butter with one hand.

"Ok, I'll do it then, it can't be too hard to make some bread rolls" He took the butter knife out of Briar's good hand.

"Thanks", Briar replied. She walked around to the front to get the cups out ready for service.

As he got to the counter, the front door swung open and her morning boys appeared, like clockwork, the muffled sound of conversation filling empty shop. Philip, as always, was leading the pack and opened the conversation with his traditional statement "Your, right" before he had made it up to the counter.

Briar really didn't want a fuss to be made and tried to angle her body so that the bloodied shirt was being covered as much as possible. She poured the coffee with her good hand and then picked up the loose change, slower than usual. By the time she had finished scooping it all in to the till, all eight guys were looking at her.

"What happened?", asked Philip in a worried tone. Briar leant over the divider and grabbed one of the bacon rolls that Jack had just put there seconds earlier. She flashed him a smile, before returning to her customers, but his back was turned on her.

"I had a slight argument with a milk bottle and a chair," Briar answered, trying to put a funny spin on the events. Jack, who was still in the kitchen, washing up the bacon tray, was listening to the conversation intently.

"Are you ok?" Philip asked, as he took the coffee from the counter and put his bacon roll in to his work overalls'. "Do you need to go to the hospital?" He leant forward to try and get a better look at the wound. That was when the guy with the split lip jumped in to the conversation.

"I can run you down there, if you want me to" He manoeuvred his body to the front of the line. As the position of the boys shifted, Briar could see Shaun, yesterday's absent mouth. She was also able to identify him from the big plaster that he had stuck on the side of his head. Briar was guessing that the tattoo removal would have been painful, but she didn't really feel like asking about it. Still filling up coffee cups, she tried to brush off his comment quickly.

"Oh, no I'm fine thanks," as she placed his coffee in front of him and leant back to grab the bacon roll.

"It needs to be properly dressed or it can get infected," he replied, not picking up the coffee. As Briar put the bacon roll on to the counter, she tried to hide the pain that had just shot down her arm. When she looked down the cloth was turning an even darker and darker shade of red.

"Come on", said the guy with the split lip and the baseball cap, "I will drop you off at casualty".

Briar didn't want to draw attention to Jack, as she didn't know what to introduce him as. Her friend? Her boyfriend? Probably more accurately, her knight in shining armour who had banded in to save the day, but she didn't have a choice.

"No, its fine," began Briar. She tried to shift her bad hand so it sat slightly straighter on her body. When she took her hand away though, it was smudged red and even more painful. Jack appeared from the kitchen, with a fresh tea towel, and the boys watched the exchange as if it was a piece of immersive theatre, being performed just to them. Jack carefully peeled her wrist away from her skin, to reveal a growing blood stain and put the fresh tea towel over her chest. He then wrapped it round her wrist tightly, before stepping back.

"I'll finish serving. Why don't you go and grab your coat from upstairs?" He stepped up to the counter to take the £5 note that had been discarded there. His left hand had brushed the side of her cheek and she smiled as she gave out instructions.

"Thanks, its £3 each for a roll and a coffee" As she walked back to the kitchen, Briar was aware that seven sets of eyes were watching her. Philip, however, had his hand in his overalls and was trying to fish out the bacon roll.

"Who are you?", asked the guy with the split lip, taking the coffee and roll. He didn't move to the side though to let the next guy get his breakfast.

"I'm Jack," he replied, putting the change on the counter, grabbing the money from the guy next to him and placing one of the bacon rolls in his open palm.

The guy next to him had a bruise on his left cheek bone and looked like he could take down a grizzly bear, if he needed to. "Move Noel" he stated, as he addressed the guy with the split lip. Noel looked at the grizzly bear man and moved out of the way to sit on the sofa in front of one of the bookcases.

Jack worked quickly through the rest of the customers, who all sat in silence and ate as Jack went in to the kitchen to get milk for the tea that one of the workmen had ordered. Jack didn't know that that was unusual for them to sit and eat. They usually all left after the last guy had been served; however, today, the mood in the shop was tense.

Noel, the guy with the split lip, got up from the sofa and walked towards the counter. Jack who had his phone out, was texting his boss at the depot, to say that he hadn't run off with the milk cart and wondered if anyone could pop up and collect it from outside Briar's shop.

"Who are you then, Jack?" asked Noel, as he placed his left fist on the counter. Showing a dodgy looking tattoo on his middle finger that sort of looked like a stretched mermaid.

"I'm a friend of Briar's," replied Jack, squaring up his body to face Noel's. Jack was trained in armed combat and didn't shy away from intimidation, but he didn't completely understand the level of hostility that he was getting from Noel.

"I'm guessing that it's your float outside then"

"Yes", replied Jack. He shifted his weight, so he felt more grounded and ready to react in case a fist came flying out at him.

"What's, it like being a milkman?" asked Philip, who had some tomato ketchup on his face.

"I like it", replied Jack. Just as Noel went to say something else, the sound of the door shutting could be heard coming from the kitchen. Briar walked in, holding her bomber jacket.

"Just make sure she gets that arm seen to" Noel said to Jack, as he turned to walk out of the shop.

The rest of the lads followed suit and for the first time since they had been coming in, in the morning. They left dirty napkins and empty coffee cups on the table.

"Everything alright" inquired Briar as Jack took the key out of the till and handed it to her.

"Yeah, fine," replied Jack "How are you feeling?" trying to push the different thoughts of what kind of relationship Briar and Noel had to the back of his head.

"Taxi," asked Briar, as the front door to the shop opened again. She turned to ask the customers to leave, but the guy standing there was holding a fast food bag and munching on some chips.

"Hey," he addressed Jack in a knowing tone.

"Hey," Jack replied looking slightly puzzled, catching the keys that the unknown man had lobbed at him.

"Trade," he replied. Jack took out his milk float keys and threw them in the air for the guy to catch. As he did, he turned around and walked out of the shop without another word.

Briar looked at Jack for an explanation as to what had just happened.

"That's my brother, Harry" offered Jack "He's gonna drive my cart back to the depot and we're gonna take his car to the hospital." Briar liked this 'take charge' attitude she was seeing and looked Jack up and down. For a second, she didn't feel the pain from her wrist. Jack took the jacket from her and placed it around her shoulders. As they walked to the front door she looked at the sign on the window. It was still displaying closed, so she there was no need to change it. Briar tried not to think of the amount of money she was going to lose by shutting the shop. As they got in to the car and headed off to the hospital, Briar looked at Jack and she could feel her stomach full of butterflies.

CHAPTER 6

The front door squeaked, as Jack held it open for Briar, then purposefully he shut it behind them both before locking it and stopping the closed sign from swaying. There had been three ladies, waiting outside the shop, moaning that it was closed, when Jack had parked up with Briar in the front seat. They had all watched as Jack had opened the passenger side door for her, but as none of them had spoken, Briar had decided that she wouldn't explain that she wasn't going to be open immediately, she thought the blood on her top did that for her.

Jack put Briar's keys on the counter, shook off his coat and lobbed it on to the table nearest one of the bookcases. Her lips were still tingling from the kiss, the first kiss that they had shared a couple of hours earlier. Briar had been seen by the nurse and then two separate doctors, before being shown in to one of the private rooms on the side of the big casualty department

She had been sitting up on the bed with her legs over the side when Jack had kissed her. Her arm was in a sling and the mascara had run down her left cheek. The doctor had confirmed that there was no glass in her arm, stitched her up and dressed the wound with a long bandage, that kept her wrist from moving freely. Jack thought that she looked beautiful and had seized the moment before his courage had left him

Driving back to the shop had felt slightly awkward in the car. The radio was broken and the two miles between the hospital and the shop felt like a long journey. Neither of them mentioned the kiss.

Getting back in the shop though she breathed in the smell of desiccated coconut. As she passed the new pile novel submissions, that she had brought down from the flat this morning. She checked the area around it to make sure that she had thrown away all the packaging. Counting the bound stacks of paper, she sighed and thought that she was too tired to read any of them now. The top novel was 'Impact', the one she had started in the bath the night before and thought back to the warning on the front page. The question 'how much attention do you pay to the people around you?' popped in to her head. She turned round to see Jack, looking at the array of cakes in the display cabinet. She noticed the bacon tray that had been washed up and was now dry on the draining board. Jack had also put away the bread and replaced the butter in the fridge.

She turned and smiled at him, as he pulled a chair out and asked, "Do you want a tea" in a slightly tense tone. His knight in shining armour routine was over. The damsel in distress was safe and home. It was 11am and Jack was very grateful that he had decided to take the long way back to the depot. He felt like he knew Briar would have tried to muddle through the morning service, without going to the hospital and seeking medical attention.

Or worse, he thought of the thug with the split lip, Noel, would have been the one to look after her and it could have been him here now instead.

Briar looked at him and smiled sweetly, before asking, "Shall we have a tea upstairs?" in a very innocent way.

Jack automatically pushed in the chair he had just moved and nodded like a giddy school boy.

"One kiss and you're already asking me up upstairs," he remarked on reaching the doorframe of the kitchen.

"Don't go getting any ideas now," she replied, without missing a beat. "It's just, that I really want to take my shoes off".

She picked up the apricot tea caddy and headed through the kitchen to the back wall, where the door to the stairs was located. She used her good hand to turn the top lock on the door. She always kept it locked, when she was in the shop, as she didn't like the idea of anyone going up there. It had become her haven since her mother's death and Jack was to be the first visitor upstairs that wasn't the boiler repair man. Briar had even been able to lock the door that morning, when she had rushed upstairs to get a jacket, before she had left Jack with her morning boys.

Heading up the stairs, Briar was aware that he was very close to her bottom, which was visible, as she had on her short puffer jacket and, luckily, her good jeans, that showed off her slight size 8 figure. She tried to walk up the stairs without wiggling her hips too much.

Jack, however, was so aware that he shouldn't be staring at her bottom, that he was examining the different pictures on the walls. The walls were a warm yellow. Briar had hung about 12 pictures in red picture frames. There were a few from her university days and the only picture Jack had ever seen of her mother, Rose, who was looking a proud as punch, standing with Briar in her graduation dress robes, her arm tucked round her daughter's waist. Both had a big smile on their faces looking at the camera.

As they ascended the stairs, there was another picture of her and a boy dancing. It was clear from the photo that they were rocking out and had no idea about the camera. At the bottom of the picture someone had put the ticket stubs in the frame. They were rock concert tickets and were about 9 months out of date. Jack had a slight pang of worry- Who was this boy? Was it an ex-boyfriend? When did they break up? Was she on the rebound?

She broke his train of worry, as she stopped at the top of the stairs. Jack had to use the bannister to stop himself from headbutting her shoulder blades.

They ended up with Briar being one step ahead of him, so they were the same height. She turned, being very careful of her arm. The last thing she needed was to end up toppling down the stairs and injuring them both further.

Jack had the thought she was going to ask him to leave. She leant in and kissed him. If you had asked Jack how long the kiss had been, he would have had no idea. Jack's thoughts about the boy in the photo melted away. She let out a small hum of appreciation and turned left at the top of the stairs, heading in to the living room. Briar became very aware that the flat was small. However, it didn't feel cramped, unlike it did when she shared it with her mother. Having Jack there made it feel nice and homely.

Briar always kept a tidy flat, so there were no embarrassing things strewn across the floor. She got naked in any room in the house, but she always tidied up whatever she disrobed. She turned to face him again in the living room and he stopped in the door frame to the room. Jack quickly took in the surroundings before he returned his focus to Briar. There were two brown two seater sofas that flanked the old television. This had a layer of dust over the screen and with the main light on it looked rather grubby. The television remote was resting on the coffee table, along with a couple of books, a laptop and the monkey nut pot with a USB stick in it. There was also an unpublished novel submission, which had a bright yellow post-it note with some writing on it. There were a couple of coffee mugs on the table; one held the remains of a cup of coffee and the other one of which was being used as a planter. There was a small, furry cactus growing out of it and a single purple flower on the tip. The coffee table was old wood and had a couple of stains on it. The table sat on a long-haired cream rug and was the fluffiest Jack had ever seen outside of a doctor's room magazine. She moved to the sofa on the left and gestured to the opposite one.

"Please" She sat down opposite him.

The tea caddy was on the sofa next to her and then moved to the back of the sofa, as she took her shoes off with her good hand.

Jack sat down and whipped off his trainers, without touching the laces. He placed them under the coffee table and his fingers brushed against the rug. He was right, it was very soft.

Briar looked at him and then said "I'm gonna get changed"

"Ok," he replied as she got up with the tea caddy still on the sofa.

"Do you want me to do anything" he asked as he went to stand up. Jack meant like make a drink or something but got embarrassed in case it came out as 'would you like me to help undress you'

Briar giggled and then smiled "No, you stay, chill out. You have had quite a morning" as she walked through to the bedroom to get changed.

Jack looked at his watch. It was 11.12am. He briefly thought about his brother and the need to return the car. He checked his phone, but there were no messages from him so he put his phone on the coffee table.

He looked at the posted note and picked up the bound paper. The post-it note had something scribbled on it, but Jack couldn't read it. So, he opened the first page and began to read....

The shadow of the man was projected on to the back wall. He avoided the burner light in the centre of the film set and the CCTV camera that was on the ceiling. He looked around the set, trying to find a suitable hiding place. He slipped his hand in his pocket and his fingers found the wet paper. He pulled it out and automatically held it at arm's length. The smell filled the room and it made the man wretch slightly. He lifted the mattress on the bed and unwrapped the paper. The smell got even stronger. There were three fish heads in the paper. He threw them onto the centre of the bed frame and dropped the mattress down. He then adjusted the duvet and began to retrace his steps, back to the door. Once he got outside, he filled his lungs with fresh air. The sound of a car started and pulled up outside the building. The man got in, adjusting his coat as he sat down. The driver in the front seat looked at the man through the rear-view mirror, patiently waiting for direction. The man finally spoke, ' Home please'. 'Yes sir', replied the driver and put the car in to drive and headed for the gate house. He stopped at the barrier and waited for the guard to get off his butt to come and check the car. The guard bypassed the driver and went straight to the back window. It was the main perk for working at the film studio. You got to talk to the movie stars and there was no one bigger than Max Thacker the....

Briar walked out of the bedroom and in to the living room, now wearing a pair of loose jogging bottoms and bright orange jumper. But Briar had hurt her arm, getting her bloodied top off, and she thought the baggiest thing possible would prevent more pain.

"Tea?" she asked as Jack looked up. She realised immediately what he was reading and was unsure if it was a good thing or not.

"Please," he replied with a smile and then returned to try and find his place on the page. She turned on her heels and walked out of the living room, grabbing the tea caddy as she left.

....star of the silver screen. Max waved but didn't wind down the window. The guard waved back and after it became painfully obvious that he wasn't going to get to talk to him, the guard sloped back to his booth to raise the gate, so that they could get out. The drive took about twenty minutes and he was used to it, having worked at the studios numerous times before on both major movie hits and box office flops. Once home, he got straight out of the car and without a word to the driver, he let himself in to the front door of his mansion, heading up to the master bathroom to run himself a hot bath and get any residual smell off his skin. Max was 47 years old, even though he looked a lot younger. His youth got him employed and now that he had such a good reputation, he had to do all that he could to protect it. The...

"Damn it", echoed through the flat.
Jack dropped the book back on the coffee table and headed through to find Briar.

"What happened? You ok? Are you bleeding again? Have the stitches come out?" By the time he had finished the last question, he had found Briar in the kitchen, her arm out of view, hidden by the worst jumper Jack had ever seen.

She was holding the caddy in her good hand and only then did he see the tea that had been strewn all over the floor. Briar had tried to open it, when she had lost control and it had gone everywhere. Jack hadn't looked in to Briar's kitchen, when he walked in to the flat. The floor was black and white checked laminate. The wooden cupboards were painted with a faded lilac and the light brown wooden counter tops were slightly lower than normal.

Jack looked back at Briar and her eyes had turned glassy. She had started to cry silently. Completely disregarding the tea, Jack bound over to her and with full awareness of her injured arm, embraced her; this made her exhale and the crying intensified.

"What's wrong?" he asked, conceded as Briar nuzzled in to his chest. One of Jack's hands was on the small of her back and the other on the back of her head. He leant back on to the counter top and Briar shifted her body so they remained together. They just stood there, Jack rubbing the small of her back, as she continued to wet his t-shirt with her tears.

They stood there for a good 10 minutes before he spoke again.

"Briar", testing the water to see if she was ready to talk or if there was going to be more crying involved.

After the long embrace, Briar disengaged herself from Jack's arms and simply said

"I spilled the tea" before laughing at the statement.

Jack responded completely sincerely with a smile "Well at least it's not your way of cleaning" He drew her in for another hug.

She giggled and wiped her eyes on the sleeve of her own jumper. "You're funny," she said getting the reference.

She looked at Jack and then at his chest She had cried off most of her makeup and it had found its way to his top. Jack noticed it as well and grinned. "Maybe I should make the tea?"

"OK" she said as she walked over to the opposite side of the kitchen and sat on the counter. Something that she had never done before in her own house. Her mother would have thrown a fit, if she had walked in to the kitchen and found Briar sitting on her work tops and as Briar barely spent any time in the kitchen the idea to sit would never have occurred to her when she was on her own.

Jack scooped up the dustpan and brush from next to the door and began to sweep up the tea from the floor.

"You didn't have plans, did you? Today I mean", inquired Briar, as she took the Orange jumper off and lobbed it on top of the fridge. There were ten or so scarves and hats on there and the large jumper encased them all. After checking on them for a second, to make sure that they didn't fall off and create more of a mess, her attention returned to Jack. He had finished sweeping up and stood up to face her before her answered.

"No not really", he said reacting to Briars gesture of where the bin was. As he threw the tea away, he noticed the whiskey that was behind the sink.

"A girl after my own heart," he remarked as the kettle boiled.

"How about normal tea?" he asked, as he threw two English breakfast tea bags in to the two mugs and poured in the hot water before adding milk. This was a small sin in Briar's eyes, but with all he had done for her in the last six hours, she was willing to let it slide. Once the tea's had been mashed, Jack picked up both mugs and followed her in to the living room.

Briar picked the sofa on the left, which meant that Jack sat back down where he had been before.

"I hope you don't mind?" he asked as he put the mugs on the coffee table. "I had a look at this one," gesturing to the novel he had started to read. Briar's knot returned to her stomach, but this time it didn't feel like a happy knot in her stomach, rather a lump like a rock.

"What did you think?" she asked, as she picked up her mug and rested it on her knee.

"I liked what I read, but I didn't understand what he was doing"

"It's had a re-write. The girl that wrote it has updated it and replaced it with the new version I didn't want to leave both version's downstairs so I bought the old one up here".

Jack nodded but, as Briar hadn't answered his question, he didn't know what to say.

"It's a sex scene," said Briar before turning red and continued, "the man, Max, he is an actor and he has to do a sex scene in the morning and he doesn't want to do it, so he plants the fish heads so it gets cancelled", she finished before taking a sip of her tea.

"Wow, it's a different idea, I would like to finish it, if I can?" asked Jack, as he took a sip of tea and burnt the tip of his tongue, trying to style it out before Briar noticed what he had done.

"So", she said. "I don't want to lie to you. I wrote it. You can borrow it, but please bring it back."

Jack looked at Briar and was about to say something, when his phone started beeping. "Sorry," he said, "it's my brother. He probably wants the car back". He got up, still holding the tea, and went in to the hallway to answer the phone. Briar, who was used to drinking very hot beverages, finished her tea, skirted past him and headed back to the bedroom.

She emerged a minute later, with a different pair of jeans on. Jack, who finished the phone call, was admiring the hall mirror.

"I should go and open the shop," said Briar, announcing her entrance in to the hall.

"Yeah you have got a bit of a queue downstairs," Jack informed her.

"Look, it's a bit embarrassing". At this point Jack kissed her again, on the mouth.

"There is no need to be embarrassed. Sod the people if they start gossiping"

Briar giggled and wiped her eye with her free hand. "No, I can't do the button up on my jeans with one hand"

"Oh," laughed Jack, as he looked down at her waist. She had put on a smaller black jumper and had her arm in a sling underneath it. She lifted the bottom of the jumper and showed the small wardrobe problem. Jack instinctively wiped his hands on his jeans, feeling how different they were, with one leg dried with milk, and carefully buttoned her jeans up. His knuckle grazed her flat stomach and he felt an electric charge of sexual energy zip through his body.

Briar dropped the jumper before she unclenched her stomach muscles, "Did you say a queue?"

"Yeah, Harry is downstairs with about ten other people, wondering if you are gonna be opening up for lunch," he answered as he grabbed his trainers from the living room.

"Yeah, I probably should actually do some work today."

"Are you gonna be ok with that hand?"

"What choice do I have?" Briar checked her reflection in the mirror. She had successfully cried off all her make-up and she still had a blotchy red neck from a slight reaction to the orange jumper.

"I could help"

"Really, you don't have to do that. I have been enough trouble as it is"

Jack thought that trying to persuade Briar might take the whole of the lunch rush, so he just walked down the stairs to the shop.

Briar watched him get about half way down before she started to follow him. She flicked off the kitchen light and then followed him downstairs.

Getting to the bottom of the stairs, Jack was already in the kitchen, washing his hands in the sink. His coat that he had left on the table was now on the back of the door. Briar looked through the shop to the front door. She hadn't noticed that it had begun to rain when they were upstairs.

"Get out some bread please. Start making up sandwiches," Briar said, as she walked out to the front counter and took the cold coffee pot from the holder, and replacing it with a clean one. She looked around the shop, as she walked towards the front door to let the people in. After flipping the sign, she unlocked it and then picked up the chair that she had knocked down earlier that morning. As she went to walk back to the counter, there were already five people in the shop. Three young business men, who had obviously popped out of the office at lunch, were there waiting at the counter, before she had made it all the way round. There were two middle aged ladies, who were sitting down in one of the corner tables and having what looked like a very polite argument.

"Hello," greeted Briar, as she checked to see what progress Jack had made with the sandwiches.

"A cappuccino and a ham sandwich," one of the business men said and then he looked over at his two colleagues, "What do you want?"

"A cheese roll and an orange juice," said the younger one. He was wearing a suit that looked like it would stand up all on its own, without a person wearing it.

"Ham sandwich and a cup of tea, Jake," the third one said.

Briar was ringing up the order, as it was said to her. She had already made the cappuccino and the orange juice.

"Two ham and one cheese please," she shouted through to Jack. He looked back at her and winked, before walking over to the front counter, pushing through the opening and continuing to work.

Briar got back in to her selling mode, as she put all the food on the tray. "Any cakes for you today?" and then remembered how heavy the chocolate cake was on the platter. Deciding that if anyone asked for it then she would have to cut it in the display case. She didn't want to worry about hurting her arm again. All three of the men looked down at the display case.

"Is that a lemon muffin?" asked the younger one.

"It's lemon and poppy seed, with lemon curd in the centre."

"Yes please,".

"Two please," the third man chimed in.

The first guy, Jake, asked for a piece of chocolate tiffin, which Briar plated up and then rang up the bill.

"Anything else?" asked Briar.

"No, that's it." said the first guy.

"£19 please" as she held out her hand, taking the £20 note that looked like it had been freshly printed. Briar wasn't used to having to do everything with one hand and she was realising how much it slowed her down. The men took the trays over to a table near to the door and the next customer stepped up to the counter, who ordered enough food to feed a family of five, before asking for a glass of tap water. Briar walked in the kitchen to get the ice for the water, as she passed on the way to the fridge-freezer. She touched Jacks waist and gave him a kiss on the cheek in appreciation for all his help. That's when she noticed the crumb on his lip. He gave her a cheeky grin, before he shoved the rest of the cheese scone in his mouth.

"Does your wrist feel ok?" he asked, as she leant down to the bottom shelf of the freezer to get the ice. Jack snatched a look at Briar's bottom before returning to look at his mound of sandwiches.

"Yeah, its fine thanks."

Briar continued to serve customers for the next hour. Jack having made a very impressive mount of sandwiches, came out to help and ended up clearing and wiping down tables. One of the customers asked if that was the new waiter, it took a second to realise the customer was Rebecca. She said Jack was just a friend helping for the day. Briar was unsure if Rebecca had noticed the fact that her other arm was inside her jumper and she had obviously damaged at least part of her body, but neither of them brought it up and so allowed Briar to serve the lady with the buggy behind her.

The lady had dirty blonde hair that had been scraped up in to a bun. The toddler in the buggy was asleep. When the lady ordered, "The biggest piece of coffee cake in the world" Briar smiled and obliged her by giving her two slices for the price of one. She decided not to mention to her that she had what looked like a couple of cornflakes in her hair. She liked this kind of customer, someone who was obviously having a very stressful time, yet she still could use please and thank you.

After the lunch rush died down, Briar found Jack loading the dishwasher. He had put the radio on and she was enjoying him wiggling his hips to the rock music. The novels, that she had bought downstairs, had moved from the central counter, to next to the serving window. And Jack was piling the clean dishes on to the island. She was thinking of shutting the shop and asking Jack if he wanted to go upstairs, watch a movie and maybe finish that kiss. But her business head was one and she knew, that she had probably lost about £200 of revenue today already.

Briar left the kitchen and dispensed two slices of Cherry Bakewell to the school girl who was waiting. She looked at the clock, it was 1.35pm. Lunch at the school must have been over, but she stood there waiting for pie. She nearly asked if she should have been in school, but noticing that Harry, Jack's brother, had finished his complimentary coffee and was now waiting to be served, Briar handed the truant the food in a brown bag and waited for Harry to step up.

"How's the injury?" he asked as he tried to look around Briar and in to the Kitchen.

"It's fine thanks, Cheers for the lend of the car" She went to the coffee maker, "Do you want another one?" She asked before she pushed the cappuccino button.

"No, I want my car keys please"

"Sure, do you want to go around?" She gestured to the open door into the kitchen. Without another word, Harry left the queue and walked in to the kitchen to find his brother.

Briar served the next two people in the queue and then saw Jack standing at the side of the counter, holding his coat.

Harry had already left the shop and was standing outside; the rain had turned to drizzle.

"I have got to go," Jack said, as he leant his head forward.

Briar kissed him on the lips "Bye," she said, before he moved her hair behind her ear.

As he left the shop, Briar noticed that the rose was still on the side of the sofa. She smiled to herself before realising that the lady in front of her was already giving her an order.

"Sorry, can you start again please?" She walked over to the till to ring it up.

"I said, a ham sandwich and a chocolate donut. And you should tie your hair up working with food!"

Briar grabbed the sandwich from the back counter and then used the long tongues to get the donut from the display case. Briar had had her hair up but had taken it down in the hospital.

"And drinks for you today?" she asked grabbing another glimpse at the blue rose.

"Milk, did you hear me about your hair?" the lady said. She was quite tall and dressed in a trouser suit with a fur coat over her left arm. She had put her designer handbag on the counter and was digging through her bag for her purse.

Briar put the milk on the tray with the rest of the order, before she answered her.

"£6.30 please" as she held out her hand "and I don't know how to tie up my hair with only one hand," Briar began, "but I will give it a go" She had delivered the statement with a deadpan expression. The customer looked slightly embarrassed and didn't reply. She just stood there, waiting for her change, before she turned and picked a table to sit at.

Briar continued to serve and clear for the rest of the afternoon. She had retrieved the rose from the sofa and it was now in the chipped vase, with the rest of the roses. Briar had even given a reprieve to the burnt orange rose but promised herself that she would bin it the next day.

At 4o'clock, a group of girl guides came in to the shop. Briar had decided that she wasn't going to try and shut today, but try and make as much money as possible. They all sat on the big sofa in front of the fire, huddled in close. There was obviously some drama unfolding, but as there was no one bleeding and no one crying, Briar hoped that she wouldn't find out what was happening. One girl was sent up, holding quite a large amount of coins. Briar got out one of the bigger trays, in anticipation for the large order.

The front door clinked open and shut again very quickly. The autumn wind was blowing quite a gale and the idea of letting the cold air in to the shop, was thought by the beret lady to be unfair, so quick as a flash, she was standing inside the shop. She adjusted her grey curls that were tucked beneath her purple beret. Once she was satisfied that she looked presentable, despite the way that the Autumnal wind blew, she joined the back of the line. As she did, she eyed up the cake selection. Having had mousse the day before, she was contemplating some sort of torte, as she moved slowly towards the counter.

She could see the proprietor serving a girl in a blue uniform and there were two men behind her, both reading the paper, as they shuffled closer to the counter.

She looked around the shop at the different customers, when a bright green cake flickered in to view. It was being devoured by a fat gentleman, who sat on her favourite crushed velvet armchair. He was reading 'The White Parrot,' The Beret Ladies favourite story in the shop to date. The man was eating the cake at an impressive rate and she hoped that he would have vacated the seat by the time she had got her order.

Throwing caution to the wind, she reached the front of the line and was met by the familiar smile of Briar.

"Good afternoon," she said in her usual cheery disposition

"Hello", replied Briar, who had clocked Beret lady as soon as she entered the shop. She had looked over to her favourite spot and estimated that her usual chair would be vacant by the time she reached the front of the line.

"Could I please try a slice of that new green cake, that the gentlemen in the corner has just inhaled" she asked, as she shook the dew off her coat.

Briar was unsure if Beret Lady was aware, or completely oblivious, of how funny she was, but Briar let out a slight giggle and touched her cheek trying to mask the noise. In doing so, she left behind a dusting of icing from the meringue that had escaped the tongs when she was fishing them out of the display case for the previous customer and had fallen on the floor.

"Yes of course," she replied, "It's key lime shortcake, a new recipe, it's going down quite well I must say," Briar stated in a proud manner.

"Could you please recommend a fruit tea to go with it?" She watched Briar take a door stop wedge size slice from the display case and place it on the tray.

"And would you like a pot of tea with that?" enquired Briar, with her good hand on the blue spotty teapot that was the closest to the front of the counter. Briar had remembered that Beret Lady had once said that her favourite colour was blue and she always tried to give her blue crockery, whenever was possible.

"Of course, dear," she replied, with a big smile. She thought to herself that she had just asked for a recommendation, but assessing that the lady was obviously injured in some way, she wouldn't bring it up and simply said, "but I would be very grateful if you could recommend one that complimented the cake" Beret lady always was very well spoken, very specific when she asked questions, as if she was a lawyer in a previous life and was used to closing all loop holes of miscommunication when speaking.

There was second where Beret Lady contemplated continuing to talk and say how much she loved the peanut butter mousse with the rose petal tea she had yesterday whilst finishing a rather arduous story about a couple who were looking for the perfect fishing spot.

"Well normally, I would suggest lime tea," said Briar, returning the smile "however, I know you're not a fan of that one. So, I think the strawberry is lovely," She put the china tea cup on the tray, next to the shortcake,

"Sounds lovely" She looked round for somewhere else to sit.

Briar noticed where she was looking, "I do think your favourite spot has become available," with a head nod to the velvet armchair that had just been vacated by the fat man. "I will come and clear the pots away in a second"

That was the icing on the cake for Beret Lady and she handed Briar a £10 note, with a big smile on her face. As usual, this is where she asked the same question that she did every day.

"Have you had anything new in?" She indicated the books.

Briar, not wanting not to disappoint the most loyal customer, was happy that's she could say yes. "I have only read the opening bit but it seems good". She thought back to the previous night, when she was in the bath reading 'Impact'

Briar reached through to the stack of unread novels that she had opened early that morning, grabbed the top one and put it on the tray underneath the shortcake. Briar had bought the pile downstairs that morning, hoping to read a bit more of 'Impact' and make a dent in the other books that had been delivered. However, the dramatic turn of events had meant that she hadn't even thought about the pile she was going to have to work through later tonight.

"Thank you," she said and went to claim her favourite vacated seat, where she nestled in to her second home and put the tea bag in the hot water to brew.

Briar was happy that she had been able to please Beret lady and moved swiftly on to her next customer, not even glancing across to see how big the line was. "Good afternoon and welcome to the unpublished teashop. How may I help you?". Briar said, getting the tray ready. Her question was met with a very grumpy looking school girl with a large fringe. She was holding a school satchel that said, 'St Jude's Catholic School' and a gym bag that looked like it had been used as the ball for a game of football.

"I want a tea and that" replied the girl, pointing to the large Bakewell tart in the display case with a clenched fist.

"Great what kind of tea would you like?" Briar asked, trying to keep upbeat, however swiftly developing an edge to her voice.

"Tea, like, human tea". Retorted the girl not breaking eye contact.

"Okay, is that for one?" The edge in her voice getting sharper with every syllable. Her wrist was starting to hurt again. The painkillers that the hospital had given her had worn off and it felt like someone was sticking a blunt fork in to her skin.

"No, there are three of us", the girl relied, glancing back at her companions who had settled at a table for four people, near the unlit fireplace. She rolled her eyes in annoyance, but luckily for the girl, Briar missed that, as she put down the small tea pot and picked up the bigger one.

"Is that three slices of Bakewell tart? Or just the one?" She positioned the cups on the tray next to the tea.

"I don't want a slice, I want the whole thing. Bring it over, we'll be sitting over there" she gestured over to near the fireplace and put a £20 note on the counter.

Not liking her attitude, Briar had reached her limit and was not going to let her get away with the rudeness. She summoned up her strongest voice and replied "Excuse me this is not a service teashop. I have a long line of customers. I will prepare it here and you will take it to the table. Do you understand?" Briar placed her hand on her hip and adopted the power stance. She was quite proud of the fact that she hadn't sworn at the customer and decided to leave out the fact that she wouldn't possibly be able to carry a tray over with only one hand.

At this point the teenager's friend came up. She was also wearing the same colour uniform and asked, "What's taking so long"? however this teenager had a skirt on instead of trousers and had left her bag where they were sitting.

"I've got to carry it to the table, apparently," offered the girl in explanation. There was no hint of trying to hide her annoyance at the situation.

"That's unusual," responded the friend.

"Well this is an unusual shop," said Briar, as she got the cake out of the display case.

"I like it. It's really funky in here," the friend said and flashing a smile of approval at Briar, she caught her eye and Briar returned the smile.

"Well you wait for it then," said the girl with the fringe and she stomped off, throwing herself in to one of the chairs and causing it to scoot backwards and hit the side of the bookcase. She had left the money on the counter, which Briar picked up and put in the till.

"God, she is being a bitch today" replied the other girl, in a very matter of fact tone, "Usually, she really is lovely, she's just having a very bad day, I am really sorry". She offered as way of explanation of her friend's behaviour.

"It's fine," replied Briar, as she finished getting the rest of the tray ready for the girl to take.

"Hi Tim," Briar said to the next customer in the line.

"Afternoon Miss B," he replied and touched his hard hat in acknowledgement.

"Usual?" she enquired, putting cream back in the counter fridge

"Please" He adjusted his belt buckle and the fat, that had been hanging over his work jeans, had been re adjusted under the belt.

"OK. That is your change, the cake and I put a dollop of cream on there as well" said Briar to the teenager with a smile. "Tell her to cheer up, almost anything is fixable".

"Thank you," she replied and cautiously weaved her way to her friends and put the tray down on the table between them. They began their own little discussion, however, Briar, with the queue getting longer, felt the need to use the bathroom return. The troubles of the teenager were pushed out of her mind.

"What happened earlier?" asked Tim, as he took the coffee from the tray and licked up the layer of foam that was on the top of it, "You were shut"

"Yeah had a little……mishap"

"Holy shit!" exploded Tim, that made the lady behind him take half a step back and watch the side of his face intently. "Where's your arm?".

Briar laughed as he put the two ham sandwiches on the same plate, "It's still under here". She pulled on the jumper "Had an accident and had to go to casualty" she explained, as she filled up a small pot of milk

"What happened?" He grabbed a bit of ham that spilled over the side and popped it in to his mouth.

"I sliced my wrist open with a milk bottle" Briar rang up his order on the till.

"On purpose?" He asked, slightly wearily.

"No of course not, you donut" She handed him the change.

Briar didn't think about the way she was talking to a customer, but Tim was sort of an unusual friend. He had had a fling with her mum a few years ago, but nothing had really come from the coupling. He called her Miss B and came in at least once a day for the same order.

"You been sniffing something stronger maybe?" he asked as he picked up the tray of food.

Briar was half way through her 'Hello' with the next customer, when she said, "What?" to Tim, who had moved out of the way.

The lady behind Tim, who looked very happy that she had reached the front of the queue, answered, "You have got some white powder on your face."

Briar pulled out her mobile phone and used the camera to look at herself

"Shit!" she said when she looked at her reflection. She let out a big sigh and the customer asked, "Long day?" with a smile and a head tilt.

"Eventful day," Briar replied, "What can I get you?"

"Black coffee and a plain cookie please"

Briar left the icing sugar on her face and took payment from the lady, who put £5 on the counter and a couple of coins in the tip jar, at the front of the till. She poured the coffee up to the top of the rim and put a lid on very carefully.

Briar served three customers, before she noticed Carol standing at the edge of the counter.

"Been in a fight?" Carol asked, as she grabbed a couple of smarties out of the jar on the back counter. Briar used them to decorate ice cream milkshakes that had been popular in the summer.

"Hi", Briar replied "yeah a bit" She pushed the tray of cakes to the customer and said, "£18.30 Please"

The woman held out her debit card and looked at Briar.

"Cash only" she said and pointed to the blackboard behind her. The blackboard was blank, Briar remembered that she hadn't written on it again after cleaning off the 'Baby Boy' sign from the baby shower.

The woman turned around. She looked like she was heading out the front door, but stopped before the door and leant over to talk to another lady, who Briar guessed was her sister. The other lady reached in her bag and instead of taking money out of her purse she handed over the whole purse and returned to her phone. The lady walked back to the front of the queue and asked, "How much?"

Briar who had been listening to the two ladies in the queue behind her whom both wanted a chocolate donut, put the donuts on two plates and replied "£18.30".

Briar stood there as the lady counted out the coins from the purse. Briar took the coins, but as it was too much for one hand to carry, put it all on the counter and begun to pick out the pound coins.

The lady huffed and then said, "It's all there," before picking up her tray of food and heading back to her table.

Carole walked up behind Briar, "I'll do that, you go for a wee" as she started to count the money quickly.

"How….?" began Briar, as she watched Carole finish counting the money and pop the till.

"You are dancing around like no one's business. Either you need the loo or you literally have ants in your pants!" She looked at the next lady in the queue, who wanted the donuts and said, "Any drinks".

"Thanks" Briar said, walking through to the kitchen and up the stairs and enjoying the silence after the connecting door shut behind her.

CHAPTER 7

After she had finished in the bathroom, Briar realised that she had the same problem as before. She couldn't do her jeans up. pulling the jumper, it came past her bottom and reminded herself not to lift for anything high in front of customers. The last thing she needed was a reputation, as a girl who flashed her knickers at customers. Briar wandered into the kitchen and opened the medicine cupboard. She looked around but couldn't find any pain killers. Grabbing the whiskey bottle from behind the sink, she knocked back two gulps and began to cough. She replaced the bottle, putting the open top on to it. As she headed back downstairs, she thought that she literally had had nothing to eat that day and was running on two cups of tea and whiskey. Briar found Carol in the main part of the shop, collecting empty plates and cups in one of the big washing up bowls. She watched her for a couple of seconds, before grabbing a cheese toastie from the freezer and lobbing it under the lit grill. As there was no queue, she put the remainder of the cheese scones in to one of her Mrs Hollis Jr, assigned Tupperware boxes, ready for the party, apart from one that she put in a plastic display bag along with a handful of sweeties. Carol walked in to the kitchen and placed the bowl in front of the dishwasher.

"You gonna be alright?" asked Carol as she looked at her watch. Briar mirrored her. It was 5.34pm, time for them to start taking in all the flowers from the street before the shop closed.

"Yes thanks, Carol, you're a star," she replied, walking to the bag of goodies on the middle counter.

"Well with no one to serve, I wasn't gonna just stand there like a lemon". She headed for the doorway in to the shop.

"Here you go," said Briar, as she scooped up the sweets with the cheese scone in the bag, "something for you to munch on driving home".

Carole took the bag, gave Briar a friendly peck on the forehead and a wave of her empty hand before leaving like a whirl wind, inspecting the goodie bag.

Briar and Carole had an unusual friendship. They were very different types of people and Briar always would describe Carole as someone who didn't mess around. She believed that she always knew where she stood with Carole. A bit like a child, if she was happy, tired or annoyed, you knew about it and there was no way you could get her to do something that she didn't want to. But Briar knew that Carole was fiercely protective. She would punch someone for you, but if you didn't see her for months, she would never take it to heart.

Briar took a deep breath, mentally searching for the smell of desiccated coconut, but all she could smell was burnt cheese. She grabbed the tongues from the side of the grill and put her breakfast, lunch and dinner on to a plate. Briar's cheese toastie consisted of mature cheddar cheese on whole wheat. She flipped it, so the burnt side was touching the plate, as she grabbed a small pot of homemade coleslaw from the fridge. Her grandmother's recipe and the one thing that was always guaranteed to be in her fridge. Her mum used to joke that If they ran out of coleslaw, then England would fall. She poured herself a cup of coffee from the pot on the front counter and stood there with her food. Glancing up to check that there was no one there to make an order, she bit in to the toastie. That was when her body realised how hungry it was.

She could smell the onions from the coleslaw, but she could still taste the whiskey in her mouth. Taking a second and third bite, she felt her stomach lurch as the food hit it. She glanced out at the shop again and caught Purple Beret Lady's eye, who seized on the connection, shooting out of her seat, making a b-line for Briar.

Briar noticed that she had eaten about half of her dessert and wondered if she didn't like it.

Beret lady was holding an unpublished book, as she walked up and did not look happy. 'Excuse me,' she said coming to a halt and leaning on the counter. Her bracelets jangled as she put her hand on the freshly wiped counter.

"This is not appropriate," she said, holding her purse in her right hand and the novel that Briar had given her in her left

"What isn't?" Briar asked, assuming she was referring to the fact that she was eating while she was supposed to be working. She covered her mouth with her good hand, trying to swallow her mouthful of food in a subtle and graceful manner.

"This book!" she replied, waving it in front of Briar's face, before plonking it back on the counter.

Briar recalled handing her 'Impact' earlier and assumed the tone of the novel had taken a sharp turn downwards. But not wanting to assume she knew what Beret Lady was talking about, she asked.

"Why not' trying not to make the end of the sentence sound so stupid. Briar glanced down at the front page and read the front cover upside down

'THE LONG GOODBYE'

Briar re-read the title and the look of confusion spread across her face. She had grabbed up the top novel and it was supposed to be 'Impact'.

Briar walked round to the kitchen and up to the pile of unchecked novels. The top one read 'Casting Couch'. She pushed it to the side. The next one was 'A Harrowing Event,' then underneath that was 'Impact'. There was a smudge of butter on the front cover.

Briar stood there, stunned for a second. She had given her best customer a novel without knowing anything about it. Briar took a deep breath and braced herself for the awkward conversation that was to follow. As she walked back, she tried to figure out how she had got the novels mixed up. Briar was sure that she had checked the title before handing it over.

"I'm sorry," she began, "I gave you the wrong one" reaching for the novel. Trying to not think about how much her wrist hurt, or how hungry she was.

"Do you know what that is" asked Beret Lady, her expression turned from anger to concern as she pointed at the novel she had been reading.

Beret Lady noticed the pain that was showing on Briar's face, glancing down at her injury. She took a deep breath to calm herself.

Briar decided to be honest "No I haven't read it."

"It's a suicide note," Beret Lady said bluntly. A lady had come and stood in the queue behind her. It was the friend/sister of the woman who tried to pay on her card. She had been on her phone when the word suicide was said. Her face snapped up and she was listening to the conversation unfolding in front of her.

"What?" said Briar. She was looking at Beret Lady but the other lady spoke

"Can I have the wifi password please?" She looked between Briar and the Beret Lady.

"We don't have wifi," Briar replied, as she flipped 'The Long Goodbye' book around so that it was the right way up and opened the front page.

"How far have you read?" asked Briar "Is it just a novel written about a suicide?" she offered. She could feel her heart pounding against her injured arm. Briar had come over in a cold sweat. She licked her lips and could still taste the alcohol mixed with the onions.

"No," she replied "they have taken the suicide note from the new Andrew Harmon novel. The opening scene".

"So, it's just a plagiarised piece of work?" Briar asked, still embarrassed that she had put something in the shop that wasn't appropriate, but happy that someone wasn't planning on killing themselves.

The Beret Lady was getting annoyed that she wasn't making her point and Briar could see that.

"Ok," Briar began, her head was spinning with different thoughts. "We close in about an hour" She looked to the queue that was forming behind her. "Why don't you go and finish your cake?" Once we are shut, I will come and talk to you about this properly, she added with a distressed smile. Briar was looking intently at Beret Lady, hoping that she would say agree.

Beret Lady nodded and without a word, she scooped up the book and headed back to her seat.

Briar found it hard to focus for the last hour of work. She tried to clear as many tables as she could, but working with only one hand, she was feeling tired. Every so often, she glanced over at Beret Lady, who was now making notes on the novel.

The last customers to leave the shop were the three girl guides, who had successfully annihilated the Bakewell tart cake. The grumpy one now had a smile on her face and they all shouted thanks to Briar as they left the shop. Briar was running a load through the dishwasher as they shut the door behind them. It looked like the sugar fix had worked and she saw they were all laughing, while walking up the road. Briar flipped the sign on the door, popped the lock and went to join Beret Lady, who was now drinking a cup of very strong black coffee.

"So", she began in a very business-like sense, "the opening chapter is, as I said, a plagiarised book." Briar noticed that Beret Lady had drawn a thin red line through the front ten or so pages. "Then it starts"......she added, handing the novel over to Briar to start reading.

...Standing there thinking, 'I could end it all. I could end it all,' watching the train approach, even at such a slow speed, I would be dead in 3 seconds.
The thought entered his head as quick as a flash and exited with as much speed. The next thing, Thomas knew was that he was on the train. The low level chatter was inaudible. And above the noise, Thomas heard, 'Hello lovely, yes I'm almost home' from the packed train. Thomas searched the crowd for the voice, a young man by the sound of it, talking on the phone, but he couldn't find him in the crowd of people. ' I'm almost home' was ringing in his ears. What would've the conversation been, if he hadn't stayed on the platform? What would have happened, if he had had the feeling of bravery two minutes later, just as the train was coming around the bend. No time for doubt to creep in. No time for the feeling of sorrow, for the family that he would have left behind. The conversation would have been.

'Darling there has been a jumper on the line. I don't know what time I'm gonna get home.' I'm sorry would have been a possibility - I'm sorry, as if the unidentified man would have felt sorrow for him, or about him. Or would he? 'A man who had killed himself in a very inconvenient way. When it would be announced that the train is delayed, delayed because they don't cancel trains when blood is spattered across the front, getting up in to the wheels of the train. There would be a rippled grown along the line'. Would there be anyone who actually cared about me? A man who he could pass in the street and not look twice at -and yet there is a man there saying I'm sorry. Thomas' breath was still shallow, as a feeling of guilt came over him. The inconvenience that he could have caused, the only impact that he would have had on someone's life would have been if he had killed himself. Was that the....

Briar put down the book and took a huge sigh. She had been sitting with the Beret Lady for about twenty minutes, having flipped the closed sign on the empty shop, she suddenly felt vulnerable.

"So, the first chapter is from another novel and then the rest of the book is just different musing of thinking about suicide" Briar clarified, as she looked at the Beret Lady, who was licking the spoon from the cup of coffee that Briar had bought over for her when they had sat down to talk.

"Yes, which you could just say, it's all a bit of bad writing, with no real narrative until you get to the last bit", replied Beret Lady, with the spoon still in her mouth before adding. "I think the changing tenses" jabbing the text that Briar had just finished reading, "was him trying to hide the meaning behind the story but not really managing it".

Briar looked at her and wondered if her writing had been subjected to the same amount of scrutiny. "I worked in publishing, so I know books," Beret lady said, as she returned to the back page of the book.

Briar felt her stomach hit the floor when she heard the word 'publishing'. How the hell could she have been giving her so many books every week and she had not taken an interest in the woman who could help her get published? Briar pushed her selfish feelings aside and returned to the problem at hand. With all Beret Lady knew about books, she felt that the idea, that this was a suicide note was more credible and she started to feel even more worried. Beret Lady had stopped on the last page and Briar began to read it.

The regret of something that you didn't want. The embarrassment, when you don't get it, does not always outweigh the relief. The date was set.

For I will be received on the day of the great battle. For my Satan will be slain in to silence. The noise will cover the deed. The Archangel will take the charge and I shall break bread with all the saints.

This life has taken the soul out of me and I shall

No longer mourn for me when I am dead

Then you shall hear the surly sullen bell

Give warning to the world that I am fled

From this vile world, with the vilest worms to dwell

Nay, if you read this line remember not the hand that writ it for I love you so

That i in your sweet thoughts would be forgot

If thinking on me then should make you woe.

O if I say you look upon this voice.

Lest the wise world should look in to your moan.

And mock you with me after I am gone.

The gossip should be rife with the news. I am sorry for the scandal I tried to participate in. The deed was not mine, yet the execution was through my step.

For one will say......

Age cannot wither her, nor custom stale

Her infinite variety.

"This page reads differently from the rest of it," Beret Lady began, her pen hovering over the page, ready to correct any spelling mistakes, as if she was a teacher marking homework "I think this is the suicide" as she sectioned it off with her pen "the rest is the rambling. He has tried to be cleaver with the wording" she continued, adding in a big circle round the centre section.

This life has taken the soul out of me and I shall

No longer mourn for me when I am dead

Then you hall hear the surly sullen bell

Give warning to the world that I am fled

From this vile world, with the vilest worms to dwell

Nay, if you read this line remember not the hand that writ it for I love you so

That i in your sweet thoughts would be forgot

If thinking on me then should make you woe.

O if I say you look upon this voice

Lest the wise world should look in to your moan.

And mock you with me after I am gone.

" I don't think that I am smart enough for this," offered Briar, as she cradled her hurt wrist that was starting to ache again. Briar looked out of the window, hoping to see Jack standing out there with dinner and a hug, hoping he would ask her to snuggle down on the sofa upstairs and allow her to end a very unusual day in his arms. But, sadly, there was no Jack outside.

"Why is he being smart?" asked Briar returning her focus to Beret Lady, not caring how stupid she sounded as she re read the page

"It's Shakespeare. One of his sonnets, but he has taken out the middle bit." Beret Lady took the spoon from the cup and put it back in her mouth as she continued to explain, "It's a sonnet about suicide and that his love should not miss him, as their love is somehow tainted. "Beret Lady stopped talking and looked at Briar with an intense stare

"So, you really don't know who sent you this book then?" She said, maintaining eye contact with Briar

"No, I looked but there was no note," she said, as she looked down at her hand and then back to Beret Lady. Briar was starting to wish that she had sat in the chair opposite her and not so close.

"You got an ex-boyfriend" Beret Lady asked. The spoon was dangling out of her mouth as she flipped to the front of the book and then back to the last page.

"I don't know anyone who would have sent this," Briar replied a bit defensively.

"Well I think that we should phone the police," Beret Lady said, reaching for her coat.

"I don't know if this is an actual thing," Briar offered trying to not insult Beret Lady. "For all we know it could just be a prank!" She took a deep breath, "or it could be an author's way of trying to get noticed by someone.

Beret Lady stopped dead in her tracks and turned to Briar with a look of horror on her face. "Did you write this so that we could talk about it?" she accused Briar, as she put on her coat.

"No!" Briar replied, shocked that she had been asked this question.

"I never told you I worked for a publisher," Beret Lady continued, "what did you think that you could exploit me and I would be so impressed that I would get you a book deal?" she continued

"No," Briar repeated, staying still "I didn't write this" She stood up so they were facing each other now.

"I can't believe this!" Beret Lady grabbed her bag and headed for the door.

"I didn't write this, I don't even really understand it!"

"Oh, it was just an accident that you gave me this book," Beret Lady tried the door but it was locked before she turned back to Briar. "I know how careful you are about reading things and then, the one day that you give me the wrong book and it turns out to be this one"

Briar stood there, not moving towards the door. "It was a mistake, you were supposed to read Impact"

"Open the door!" Beret Lady demanded.

Briar moved towards the door and as she did, Beret Lady commented, "I can't believe I fell for such a scam!" Briar let her walk through it and heard her continue to talk as she walked up the street.

Briar shut the door and instead of clearing away the crockery, she sat back down and looked at the writing again. Was it a joke? She asked herself or was there really someone who had sent this in a suicide note. That would make sense. Briar, being honest with herself, hadn't really believed Beret Lady until she had been accused of this all being a hoax, but now fear was nestled at the pit of her stomach.

CHAPTER 8

It was 8.30pm and the knot in Briars stomach had grown. She was now feeling very sick in addition to the searing pain in her left wrist. The anxiety wasn't because Jack had called to say that he would be over later, but because of what Beret Lady had accused her of. She felt the need to justify that she wasn't behind the suicide note. Briar believed that if Beret Lady started to tell people she was manipulating customers, she would be out of business before the end of the year. Briar, when getting dressed this morning, had preboiled some pasta for dinner. She was planning on applying an old face mask that she had wanted to do before her scheduled meeting with Jack the next day. Briar looked down at the face mask bottle, that she had left on her make up table, and laughed at herself. She had convinced herself that the face mask was supposed to bring out the natural shine and was what would be needed to get Jack to kiss her. In fact, all she needed to do was injure herself.

Jack had mentioned that he was at the pub with his brother and was going to go to his own flat that night to pick up some things before popping over. Jack had made it very clear that this was not a booty call and that he was merely coming over to check on her. Briar wandered in to the kitchen and mindlessly opened the fridge before deciding that there was nothing in there that she wanted to add to her pasta.

Stopping dead in the kitchen, watching the pasta sauce bubble, she had a feeling of forgetfulness wash over her. She knew that there was something she had forgotten to do and ran through the plan that she had made in her mind that morning before the whole milk bottle fiasco started. She couldn't think what it was and after carefully poring the pasta sauce over her reheated pasta, making sure that the hot liquid didn't splash on to her skin, Briar had just had a bath and was now only wearing matching bra and knickers, just in case Jack wasn't feeling as gentlemanly as he had implied. Briar had no intentions what so ever of answering the door in just underwear, but her skin felt hot and prickly and she thought that she would throw a dressing gown over herself before he arrived. Sticking a fork in her mouth, she headed for the living room.

Flicking on the TV to catch the end of a house program, she began to eat her dinner. Briar noticed that one of the net curtains had been disturbed, and she thought of Jack who had been in there earlier. Her copy of the Max Thacker novel – Beginning - was still on the table. She wondered how far he had got and guessed that he probably wasn't up to the funeral scene yet. Briar was never happy with that scene and she thought back to how many rewrites she had gone through before she had given up on it. Briar mindlessly looked over to the desk in the corner of the living room and to where she had kept copies of all the scenes that she had cut from bits of writing, as they were superfluous and didn't help move the narrative along when she remembered what she had forgotten to do.

She was supposed to be catering a funeral the next day and she had completely forgotten to do anything. She put the half-eaten bowl of pasta on top of her closed laptop and headed out of the living room. Swearing in her head as she went, swallowing the bland food. She put on a pair of shorts and a tank top, grabbed her keys and the phone that she had on charge and headed down the stairs. Briar forgot for a couple of seconds that she had hurt her hand and let it fall to the side of her body. As she did the pain shot up her arm and in to her chest. She swore loudly, as she gently manipulated her wrist so that it could rest back on her boobs.

Briar searched with her foot for her flats, as she heard her phone vibrate in the central counter. She grabbed her work diary from the top of the fridge and noticed the black dot next to the next day's date. She had written the word Hillier, then the abbreviation NO AL +C, which stood for no allergies and they wanted a cake. She always offered a cake in conjunction with the funeral spread, but always made a note of whether they wanted to have it. Funeral cakes were always a tricky sell, as they couldn't be too flashy, but they needed to look tasty. Briar had managed to wash her hair with one hand and after it is blow-dried, it went all fluffy. There was no way that she could start preparing food without tying it back. She slipped off her flats and ran back up-stairs, returning seconds later with a shower cap over her head. She was shoving the loose strands of hair in to the cap that was ironically patterned with cupcakes.

She checked her phone. It was Carol, asking for a batch of those cheese scones for the next day. Briar grabbed two big mixing bowls from under the central counter and began to pour ingredients into the bowls. Briar never used scales when measuring out ingredients and supported the flour and sugar packets in the crook of her left arm. Her phone buzzed again. Carol had sent her a smiley face, followed by a picture of a jug of beer. Briar glanced at it, smiled and returned to work.

As she walked to the front counter to see how much she could steal from the display cabinet, Briar noticed Jack through the window at the front of the shop. She stood there watching him for a couple of seconds. He was on the phone and having what looked like a very heated discussion. Briar didn't want to look like she was spying, so she glanced down at the display cabinet, making a mental note of what she could use and then headed back to the kitchen.

She grabbed a couple of packets of rolls from the big bread bin and immediately decided against trying to cut them up herself. After checking on the big mixers, that were currently hard at work, she looked at the big tub of sausage meat that was at the bottom of the fridge. With an about turn, she grabbed another mixing bowl and started to add ingredients to make a pastry, wondering to herself if she would have given up trying to cut the bread or lift the sausage meat pot from the fridge if she hadn't seen Jack outside. But as she finished adding the pastry ingredients to the bowl, her phone started to ring. She looked at it and then to the front door. Jack was fiddling in his pockets and instead of answering the phone, she just walked over to let him straight in. The lights were turned off in the front of the shop and when she got to the door, Jack jumped backwards, startled by Briar's sudden appearance.

She unlocked the front door and then stepped back, allowing Jack to let himself in. He smiled a sheepish grin at his reaction to her stealthy entrance. Briar looked at Jack as she shut the door. She didn't know if she should kiss him or not.

"Hi," she began

Jack threw his bag on to the chair nearest the door and kissed her before he replied. "Hello" Jack then looked from her injured arm that she was resting on her boobs, to the tank top and the very short shorts that she had on.

Briar became very conscious that she had not that much clothing on and tried to step out of the streetlamp's light. From the window, you couldn't see anyone looking in, but her self-consciousness was picked up on by Jack and he gathered up his bag and with a guiding hand, escorted her towards the kitchen.

"How was the rest of your day then?" he asked before they reached the kitchen door."

"Eventful," Briar replied, "sadly it's not over."

Jack began to ask why, when he looked in the kitchen to see the two mixers going at full speed and the bread on the counter, waiting to be chopped up.

"You do a night shift as well?" asked Jack, as he dropped his bag next to one of the dessert fridges.

Briar expected him to look annoyed. The idea of cuddling and chatting over a beer had suddenly evaporated and the girl, whom he had started kissing only that morning, was now looking to him again for help. Briar knew that if she was in his shoes, then she would be looking for the quickest escape route possible. So, Briar decided to give it him.

"I'm catering a funeral tomorrow that I forgot about. It's gonna take me a couple of hours to get everything ready," she clarified as she checked on the mixture of the two-mixing bowls and added some food colouring to one of them. "Thanks for checking on me, but I know you have to get up super early tomorrow for work, so I understand if you want to bail". Briar held her breath and waited for his response. She knew that she had no right to expect him to stay, but she really hoped that he would.

Jack smiled at her "What do you want me to do first?" he asked, as he took off his watch and pocketed it, walking over to the sink to wash his hands.

Briar smiled and felt her eyes starting to well up. "You could cut the bread up please to make rolls". Jack grabbed the tea towel from the counter to dry his hands and went the long way to where the bread was, stopping off at Briar for a kiss. As she kissed him, she wiped a tear away from her right cheek before it touched Jack's skin.

She watched him walk over to the other side of the kitchen and she thought about the amount of times she had cried in the last couple of years. Once when her mother died and once when she had had a customer, who was the vilest human being that she had ever met. In the last eighteen hours, she had cried three times and each time it was near Jack. Briar really didn't know what was wrong with her. She just felt that she could allow herself to be vulnerable in front of him and she really didn't like that about herself. As Briar silently composed herself, when Jack's back was turned, she got the sandwich fillings out for the rolls.

"How is your wrist feeling?" Jack asked, as he swiftly got to work cutting and buttering the rolls the same as he had done at lunch time.

"Alright thanks," she replied as she got the cheese out of its bag and poured it in to a bowl, adding in the spring onion and salad cream, "It hurts a bit."

"Jagged glass met with flesh. I would be surprised if it didn't hurt," Jack said turning to face her. "More rolls?"

Briar grabbed a couple of packs of brown rolls this time, out of the big bread bin, and tossed them over the kitchen to Jack.

"You know tomorrow was supposed to be our monthly meeting" He turned and cut the rolls up, "I was looking forward to it".

"Sorry", Briar replied in a playful tone. "Do you want to go and we can flirt in a really public, awkward way tomorrow?" She picked up the sandwich filler and carried it over to Jack for him to start filling the rolls with.

"No, no definitely not," he said, smacking her bum as she walked back. "How many of them do you want?" He grabbed a spatula out of the drawer and began making up the sandwiches.

"Six white, six brown for the cheese and I will make up some ham and tomato ones as well" She checked on the mixture.

Jack set off to work, separating out the white and brown rolls, as Briar checked on the mixture. She was making cheese scones in the right-hand mixer and a sponge to chop in to iced lady fingers in the other. Using her good hand, she stopped the mixer from spinning and disconnected the bowl. She attempted to carry the cheese scones bowl over to the central counter. Jack saw that she was struggling and came over to help.

"So," he began with a smile, "were you very busy today?"

"Usual really, just it felt harder with that fact that I only have one hand" She grabbed a hand full of the cheese and worked it in to the mixture.

Briar took a second and wondered if she should mention to Jack the events that had occurred with Beret Lady, as she spooned the ingredients in to cupcake trays.

"Could you put the oven on?" she asked, as she continued to deposit the mixture. "I think I have lost one of my best customers though," Briar began.

Jack had already obeyed the command and had returned to the rolls, now cutting the tomatoes.

"Not that workman?" Jack asked, "Noel, was it?" being very careful of his tone. Jack had taken an instant disliking to him, but he didn't know the history between him and Briar.

"Who, what, no!" Briar responded, as she brought the first tray of cheese scones over to the oven and put them on the top shelf. "One of my ladies read something that she thinks is a suicide note or something, but now she thinks that I'm the one that wrote it."

Jack stopped chopping the tomato at the word 'suicide' and looked at Briar.

"So, is it a suicide note?" Jack asked, wiping the tomato juice off his hands with a tea towel.

"I don't know. Maybe someone has actually done what this lady has accused me of." She began to fill up the second cupcake tray. "I mean, apparently, this lady is some sort of big shot in the publication world and she thinks I was trying to manipulate her so maybe someone else was."

"So, what are you gonna do?" asked Jack, as he began to divvy up the ham in to the rolls.

"I don't know, I don't know if I should ring the police, or wait to see if anyone comes in asking stupid questions or just throw the book away".

"Can you trace the sender somehow?"

Briar stopped for a second to think. She knew that the packaging was long gone, "I could put a message out through social media I suppose". She thought of her online page and got embarrassed about the amount of time she had spent stalking Jack on social media. Her wrist was beginning to hurt again and her mind briefly turned to the whiskey bottle upstairs.

Briar remembered what the doctor had said to her, that this kind of cut could get infected and she should monitor her temperature. She felt her forehead and suddenly remembered the shower cap that was on her head.

"Oh, my lord!", she exclaimed as she took it off her head. "I forgot I was wearing it." She tossed it on the stool next to the back door

"I thought it looked sexy," Jack replied with a smile

"Yeah right"

"Ok no I didn't, but I guessed there was a reason behind the shower cap and I hadn't figured it out yet."

"I can't tie my hair up and I didn't want to contaminate the food," Briar explained before adding, "I feel such like an idiot." She hid her face from Jack.

"You're not an idiot," Jack counted, as he moved towards her. He stood behind her so that she wouldn't have to face her. Being very careful of her wrist, he wrapped his arms around her body and nuzzled his face in to her neck. "You are sweet," he began in a soft tone

"You are kind," he continued, as he kissed her cheek, "and you run a business all by yourself. I think that it is amazing". Briar turned in his arms and kissed him. Her good hand rested on his cheek. She could feel his soft skin.

"You shaved," she commented, not moving from his embrace

"I thought it would be weird if I brought over an electric razor," Jack answered. "To be fair, we have only had this going a day," he continued, smiling at her "If you kick my ass out now, it would be awkward to try and get my razor back."

"Always be prepared, that's your motto isn't it?"

"That's the scouts. I'm a milkman."

"You were forces though," Briar countered in a playful manner.

"How did you know that." Jack asked, looking in to Briars eyes,

"I may have seen you in a uniform" Briar confessed.

Jack smiled, kissed Briar on the forehead, breathing in the smell of jasmine and released her from his embrace

She looked over at the sausage meat tub and then said, "Do you want a beer?"

"Yes please," he replied. Briar grabbed a couple of display trays out from underneath the central counter and handed them to Jack. He took them and started to plate up the bread rolls.

Jack thought to himself that if all they could offer so far was some sandwiches and cheese scones, they would be there a long time.

Briar appeared from upstairs and shut the door with her good hand. This time however she didn't lock it.

She put the beer glass on the counter. Jack noticed the beer bottle cradled in her elbow. It was from a local brewery. Jack liked the fact that she supported the local industry and somehow the hot girl in short shorts, holding alcohol became even more appealing. Briar opened the beer using the edge of the counter and a weird wrist flip that made the popping sound when the air pressure released from the bottle. She put the bottle on the counter and remembered the other mixing bowl for the sponge fingers. Grabbing another tray, she looked over to Jack who was arranging the rolls in a pretty pattern.

"Could you?" she asked pointing to the mixing bowl.

Jack dropped the cheese sandwich that he was arranging and put the sponge mix on the central counter. "Good job I stopped by," he said, as he moved the mixer over, grabbing the beer bottle and taking a swig.

"Honestly, I half expected you to have ran out of the door by now," Briar confessed, as she got out another batch of rolls that needed cutting.

Jack didn't wait to be asked to spoon the mixture into the baking tray - he just did it, swallowing half the beer in two gulps. "Course not" he replied. "So, you thought the flirting was obvious then".

"Completely" She made up some more sandwich mix.

"So why didn't you respond to my question?" he asked, leaning back on the fridge that wobbled slightly at the amount of pressure Jack placed on it.

"What question?" Briar asked, as she momentarily disappeared in to the small pantry under the stairs. Jack could hear some banging around, coming from the pantry.

He raised his voice a bit to counter the noise, "The question on the milk bottle"

Briar reappeared with a cake tin that had a sticky label on it. It read Eggs

"Which milk bottle?" She vanished again in to the pantry

"I spelled it out every day!" Jack was starting to get a little embarrassed. "The letters on the milk bottle….. they were asking you out."

Jack was rearranging the rolls, so that they formed a different pattern on the display trays, and kept his back to Briar.

She emerged from the pantry again, this time with two cake tins and she nudged the pantry door shut with her hip.

"The letters on the milk bottle?" she queried, carefully placing the tins on the counter. They landed with a thud and Jack guessed they were filled with more ingredients. "They spelled something?"

"I thought that you would get it." The embarrassment was building in Jack and he could feel his hand start to shake. He took another swig of the beer and checked on the scones. The ones on the top shelf looked like they were about cooked. He switched them over, using Briar's monster oven mitt.

Briar looked down at the tins and tried to open them with just one hand. "I think you think, I'm smarter, than you think that I am." The tin slid out of her grip and landed flat on the floor. Jack turned around at the crash. He couldn't see Briar for a second, as she was crouched down behind the counter. He rushed round and picked up the tin for her.

A car's wheels screeched outside the front of the shop and they both looked out in to the empty shop. They couldn't see anything in the dark and their focus returned to each other.

Briar could see that Jack looked a bit sheepish and tried to console him. "I can't believe you took the time with me," she offered, as she stroked his freshly shaved cheek.

"What are you making now?" asked Jack.

"Ha ha," replied Briar. "Open these up please" She tapped on the metal tin. Jack did as he was told and saw that the first box was full of mini fruit cakes, the second with muffins and the third with scotch eggs.

"Wow a feast!" The smell of pastry filled the air.

"they were supposed to be for another customer on Saturday. I thought if I use them for the funeral, I can make more tomorrow and we can actually have an hour without food or customers…."

"Or blood," Jack offered, as he looked at Briar's wrist.

"The sponge should take 25 minutes to cook," Briar began, formulating a plan as she spoke "Why don't we plate these up on those serving trays and then call it an evening?"

"That sounds like a plan," replied Jack, as he looked at his wrist for the time, forgetting that his watch was in his jeans pocket. Jack was not going to admit to Briar that he had gotten changed a couple of times before he had arrived at her flat. He had chosen a darker pair of jeans and a black top this time, in case there were more tears that resulted in makeup stains on his top again.

Jack watched Briar artfully arranged the food on the trays, before he wrapped them up in cling film and carefully placed them in the fridge.

Jack removed the cheese scones and sponge fingers from the oven and left them to cool on the wire racks in front of the ice cream maker. Before he knew it, they were making their way back upstairs. All the lights had been turned off and the hum of the fridges could be heard through the connecting door. Jack lead the way up the stairs this time, passing the same picture of the guy that had made him feel uneasy earlier. Jack had realised that he was more insecure than what he had realised. Jack put it down to the fact that he had not really had such strong romantic feelings for someone before and he knew that he wanted things to go well. He hesitated half way up the stairs and in a moment of vanity, wondered if Briar was currently looking at his bum this time.

CHAPTER 9- Thursday

Jack stepped out of the front door of the shop. His watch told him that it was 4.13am. He was already running late and knew that he was going to have to run the two miles to work, if he was going to make it there in time for the start of his shift. Before starting the run, he looked down at his shoes to notice that one of his laces was untied. As he turned in to the light of the street lamp, he saw a shadow next to the wall at the bottom of the street. The figure was facing the wall and the image reminded him of the punishment he used to receive at school, having to stand on his own with his nose touching the wall and thinking about the naughty thing that he had done. The figure was completely still apart from their left hand, which was slowly stroking one of the plaques that was on the wall. Jack had only stopped to look at the plaques on the wall once. The great tradition of having your name put up there was a momentous achievement according to Jack's grandfather – it was for service to the town and was paid for by the grand family that lived in the manor house at the end of the street.

As he passed the figure, he could hear a voice. Jack couldn't see if he was talking to himself or if he was on the phone, but as he couldn't see his face, he didn't slow his gate as he rounded the corner to look back at the figure. As Jack weaved in to the road to avoid the parked car that had taken up the whole of the pavement, he noticed the to-let sign in the front garden of the house next to it. Jack's thoughts returned to the figure. He assumed that he was ok, as he didn't look very distressed and Jack headed off to work.

Jack thought that the most identifying thing about him was the big black jacket/ hoody type thing that had a red cross sewn in to the pattern over his left shoulder. It looked like a custom job, as far as jack could tell, and he wasn't too knowledgeable on that. He mulled the image of the figure for another couple of seconds before his thoughts returned to Briar, whom he had left sleeping upstairs in her warm bed. He had set his alarm on his phone to vibrate the night before and was really happy with himself that he managed to get up, dressed and out of the flat without waking up Briar. They had gone to bed very late the night before having stayed up with a bottle of wine and some blueberry shortcake that Jack had picked from the counter when Briar had sent him downstairs for a bottle opener. Jack remembered the model figure that he had re-covered with a sheet when he had got out of bed. She was so beautiful and yet she seemed to only eat cake and bread. Jack had been rather dumpy in his youth and had worked extremely hard to lose the extra weight, so the idea for Jack to run to work was duel beneficial. It allowed him to work off some excess calories from the shortcake and it was a lot closer to work than his house, which meant that he could spend more time snuggled up to Briar.

This was his first morning leaving for work from the tea shop; however, Jack hoped that it would become a regular occurrence. The only thing Jack wasn't completely happy with was the fact that he had had to sleep on the wrong side of the bed to normal. Briar had wanted to sleep on the left, as it meant there was less chance of Jack elbowing her injured wrist while they slept.

The memory of the feeling, could be felt throughout his body and he had gotten so distracted by his thoughts of Briar, that he had mindlessly passed his works entrance and stopped at the traffic lights to turn around and run the last two hundred yards back to work. Jack ran past the gateman and the lads that were already in their milk floats ready to go out and start their rounds. He ran in to the staff room and went straight to his locker. Within two minutes, he had got changed and was heading to his milk float that had already been stacked and charged. He grabbed his keys from the office and within five minutes, he had put down his first pint of milk. Jack knew that his rounds would take about 3 hours, but if he was very quick today, he thought he would make it back to the shop before the workmen popped in for their breakfast. Jack wasn't a man, who was used to dawdling, so the game to beat them to the shop was on.

CHAPTER 10

When Briar looked up, after replacing all the sugar pots that she had finished wiping down, she saw a customer heading down the high street, and hadn't even made it back behind the counter before the bell rang.

She noticed Jack's coat on the back of the door. He had gone upstairs to have a shower after work that morning. He had bashed in to a couple of dustbins in his float, whacked his head on the dashboard and he had a headache. It was 9am and Jack had just got back, having spent a good hour filling in 'stupid incident forms', as he had phrased it. Briar had sent him upstairs for a shower, so that he would calm down and then hopefully they could spend the morning together.

Briar stopped thinking about Jack and turned her attention to the customer.

"Good Morning, Mr Thompson," she said in her usual sing-song way.

"Good Morning dear", he replied, as he manually shut the door. It was on a spring hinge and would close by itself however the gentleman wanted to make sure that it was shut. Briar thought briefly about mentioning it again to Mr Thompson; however, with the way that the conversation had gone last time, she decided to save a good 10-minute lecture about the etiquette of making sure that doors were shut. The last time she had brought it up, she had to listen to a horror story in which Mr Thompson recounted the time that he had seen a child who had tried to sneak through a door and got their fingers caught. Briar had had a hard time making that Victoria sponge cake later that day, as the blood red colour of the Jam had made Briar's stomach churn.

"So, what can I do for you today, Mr Thompson?" She got a tray out ready for him.

"Well I would be very grateful for a cup of coffee and a piece of fruit toast," he said, his hands on the wooden counter, next to the complimentary children's lollipop's

"What's the days choice of jam?" she asked, putting the fruit bread under the small grill.

"I think we will have a bit of apricot today please," and then he took a huge sniff. "Can I smell peppermint?" he asked inquiringly.

"Yes, you have got a good palate Mr T"

"Thompson, please ducky. I'm not a character in a television show," he said with a playful scold.

"There you go then, Mr Thompson," she replied with a slight emphasis on his surname and she briefly turned back to the toaster for no reason at all, except that he was unable to see her face.

"Everything alright?" Mr Thompson asked, as he nodded at Briars wrist, once she had returned to face him.

"Yes," Briar replied moving along the counter.

"Bristol Fashion," the elderly gentleman added, which made Briar smile.

"Anything else for you?" Internally, she was weighing up the way that the day was going to evolve. Her thought was answered immediately "Actually," he continued, "could you please take for a pot of tea for two and two slices of apple crumble?....But can you bring it over once I have been joined by my lady friend?" He smiled at her, very innocently, and handed over a crisp £20 note.

Briar took the money and handed back his change. She watched Mr Thompson toddle off to the seating and wondered who he would be meeting that day. If he was 50 years younger, he would be referred to by his friends as a man – whore, meeting a different woman every week for a cup of tea and a slice of cake. Briar often gave the ladies names, such as lovely Louisa, who couldn't stop smiling throughout the whole date, or, sexy Sandra, whom was the older lady that had on a full-length leopard print coat. When she removed the coat, Briar was slightly worried that she would be required to call an ambulance to resuscitate Mr Thompson. His jaw dropped as she revealed her skin-tight white, all in one track suit. She mused at who would be the lucky lady for that day. Where did he meet all these ladies? Briar wondered, as she rolled out the puff pastry for the pastry cups that she would fill with the chocolate pudding and marshmallow crème. They were a special order for Mrs Hollis Jr.

Mrs Hollis Jr was throwing her annual party, and all the main dishes were created from scratch by herself and her friend Mrs Washer. But every year the desserts would come from Briar's kitchen. She knew full well that both Mrs Hollis Jr and Mrs Washer would apologise to their guests about not being able to sort out the desserts themselves; that they had to, at a last resort of course, turn to Briar to cobble together something palatable for the party. It was a Christian event, Briar recalled, after she had once referred to the party as a shin dig. It was to celebrate something called Michaelmas and was an event that celebrated a feast, so, Briar saw the event as a party to celebrate a party. And every year she had to stop herself from asking if she could join in, just to see how Mrs Hollis Jr would wiggle out of the invitation request.

Briar was completely aware of the situation with one of Mrs Hollis Jr's events, most of the main lunches would end up in the bin as people would politely pick at the dishes for a certain amount of time before it was acceptable to move on to the desserts. Which would get gobbled down at the first chance. The guests would be very kind and say how much they loved the salmon moose and the split pea soup with little croutons and not under any circumstances discuss the large slice of honey and walnut sponge cake with dark chocolate drizzle that was strategically placed in their jacket pocket for later. She was aware of the situation, and she took full advantage of it, when she would get the phone call from Mrs Hollis Jr. asking If she would cater the desserts she would have to listen to her go on and on about the fact that she was only asking her as a last resort. Briar would allow her to go through the rigmarole of the situation and then charge her an extremely inflated rate that she would have to pay, as she secretly knew how much everyone loved the desserts.

She always strived to deliver desserts that were better than the time before. It was also a really good way of marketing what she could do. Usually a couple of weeks after the party, she would get a hushed question over the counter about an exotic dessert that she had made up. Once she was asked by one of the predominant ladies of the town, Mrs Yeoman, who ran an online food blog, if she could borrow the recipe for a couple of weeks. When Briar offered to sell her the recipe for £200, she turned on her heels and walked her wobbly bottom out of the shop, without a word. The following month, a version of the sea salted and blackberry cheesecake appeared on the web; however, the recipe outlined far too much sea salt and Briar imagined that the dish would need to be consumed in such small amounts that it would be hardly worth making it.

Briar was walking to and from her kitchen, serving a couple of people and clearing away plates and cups that had been discarded, when the door went. She glanced up a few seconds later to see if there was anyone waiting to be served, when she caught the end of the hug of Mr Thompson and the new mystery lady. She was not a lovely Louisa or a sexy Sandra. In fact, Briar didn't want to assign a name to that lady because she looked so miserable that if she called her something, she felt that she would be doing an injustice to the other people with the same name. She named her Ms Grump, while she was kneading the cheese dough with one hand, which took a lot of effort to keep her bad wrist still, that she would later turn into cheese and chilli Jam cups. She called her Ms Grump, as she was almost certain that she would have never have been married. She was about five foot two inches, with slim legs and a rather portly belly. Her hair was black and grey and looked clean from a distance. It was the face that sold it; Ms Grump had a scowl on her that would rival the meanest of head teachers. She knew she had to stop working on the dough and would have to bring over the tea and cake that Mr Thompson had already paid for. She cleaned her hand, left the bread to rise in the bowl and sorted out the order. As Briar was walking over, she had a mental image of Ms Grump sending her to the corner, for interrupting the conversation that they were having.

Ms Grump barely turned her head, as Briar laid the tray down in between them.
"Thank you very much," said Mr Thompson, watching her movement eagerly.

Ms Grump gave a slight head tilt towards Briar, but her gaze did not leave Mr Thompson.

Briar lingered there for a moment trying to place the smell of Ms Grump's perfume; however, she couldn't place it and simply said, enjoy, turned and headed back to the counter.

Briar had perfected carrying a tray with one hand and using her hip to rest the other side of the tray on. She thought that, once her wrist had healed, she could continue to serve drinks this way, as she could use her other hand to pick up more things. As she made it round the counter, two people entered the shop dressed in all black. A tall, black gentleman with grey hair and a thin beard stood just in the door. A younger girl was standing beside him. She had on a knee-length black dress, with a high neck line and a black cardigan in her right hand. Briar knew that these was people from the Hillier family, who had come to collect the spread, that she had finished making up just twenty minutes earlier. Briar hated having to talk to people about money when they were grieving, but it was her business and she took a deep breath, as walked round the front counter to meet them. Both mourners noticed Briar immediately and met her in the middle of the shop.

"Hello," began Briar, "I'm sorry for your loss", in a completely sincere tone. She was trying to remember who the dead person was. She remembered that she had been told their name, but as she couldn't recall it, she didn't offer any other conversation.

"Thank you," the gentleman said.

"We have your cash," added the girl, who produced an envelope full of money from underneath her cardigan.

"Thank you," Briar replied, taking the envelope from the girl and slipping it in to her apron, before adding, "Will you follow me?" Briar wobbled a bit in her tone. She didn't quite know how cheerful to be. If she should try and pitch the mood down, would that be more respectful? Or should she try and ignore what they were going to have to do that day, and try and lift the mood.

They followed Briar around the counter and in to the kitchen. Before Briar could start to go through what she had made up for them, there was a knock at the back door.

"Excuse me," Briar said as she slipped past the girl and headed for the back of the kitchen. She unlocked the door and then slid across the two deadbolts that held it shut. She grabbed the handle with her good wrist and turned, but it didn't open. The knock repeated, this time with a little more force. Briar hip checked the door and then pulled hard. It opened this time and Briar was a little more than surprised to find Mrs Hollis Jr standing outside next to the bins.

"Hello," Briar offered,

"Good Afternoon," Mrs Hollis Jr responded, before walking in to the kitchen and looking around at the trays of food Briar and Jack had prepared. Briar's brain started to work overtime. Was Mrs Hollis Jr there to collect for her event as well? Had Briar got the date wrong for her order? 'Oh lord!' she thought to herself. But Briar stood there by the door, as she watched Mrs Hollis Jr walk over to the gentleman and give him a kiss on the cheek as a greeting.

"Charlotte", she remarked, as she patted the girl's hand.

Briar breathed a sigh of relief. Only now was she looking at what Mrs Hollis Jr was wearing. She was dressed in all black with a black hand bag and a black pill box hat, that was neatly resting on her hair.

Briar opened her mouth to speak, but before she could start, Mrs Hollis Jr, interjected, "The car is outside." At which point, Briar looked out the door to see a Mercedes parked next to the bins, in what used to be the loading bay for the shop next door.

Charlotte was the first one to move. She picked up a tray of sausage rolls and headed outside.

Mrs Hollis Jr ignored Briar standing there and asked the gentleman, "How are you doing?" with another pat of her hand.

The gentleman nodded with a sullen look on his face but declined to speak.

Mrs Hollis Jr either missed the fact that the man was obviously suffering or didn't care so she asked another question,

"Is the house all set up for the wake?" not moving from her spot, directly in front of the upset man.

Briar stood there trying to figure a way of getting this awful woman away from Mr Hillier, but before she could do anything, the door to the flat opened and Jack walked into a full kitchen, something that he wasn't expecting. Mrs Hollis Jr, turned away from the grieving man and analysed Jack, who had walked over to Briar.

Placing his hand on the small of her back, he asked "Shall I help?" to Briar, who had begun smiling at the appearance of Jack.

"Please," she replied, as Charlotte walked back through the door and picked up two serving trays this time.

"Hello," offered Mrs Hollis Jr, in an enquiring tone

"Hi," Jack replied, as he was half on his way out the door.

The grieving gentleman also seized on the fact that Mrs Hollis Jr's attention had been diverted and he picked up a tray of rolls, that was closest to him, and headed out to help pack the car.

Mrs Hollis Jr was left standing in the kitchen alone, not doing anything. Briar mindlessly altered the position of her wrist that had been resting on her chest, before counting the remainder of the trays, that still had to be packed into the car. Within 10 minutes, all the food had been packed away and Briar was standing with Mrs Hollis Jr in an awkward silence.

"What have you done to your wrist?" she asked in a very cold tone. Briar tried to analyse the sentence to see if there was any concern there or if she was just being nosy.

"I just sliced it open," she replied in a very matter of fact way. Then she remembered that Mrs Hollis Jr could still cancel her order and with the fact that the shop had been shut that week already, she couldn't afford to lose the money she would make from the event. Briar offered, "It doesn't hurt to much".

"Well I hope you can still make up those delicate cakes that I had asked for," she replied, referring to the sugar flowered cupcakes.

'Oh,' Briar thought, 'you couldn't care less about me, you're just worrying about your stupid party'. But taking the more diplomatic approach, she replied, "Yes, of course I can," before adding the dig, "I'm still very skilled with one hand," just as Jack walked through the door.

"They are walking back to the house," Jack offered up to the room, not quite sure whom he should be telling.

"Ok," acknowledged Briar. "I will see you on Saturday then Mrs Hollis," she continued, as she moved out of the way of the door so Mrs Hollis Jr could walk through it.
"No, you won't," she replied, as she walked towards the kitchen door, "My son is going to collect the order on Saturday".

As she looked out to the car, Briar heard footsteps heading towards the kitchen door. Carl was standing there in a black suit, with a black and red jacket over the top of it.

Briar recognised Carl immediately, but as soon as her eyes met his, he stopped walking and turned away.

"Good bye," Mrs Hollis Jr offered to the room and headed for the driver's side door. Carl didn't say anything, but stood next to the passenger door and waited until his mother had got in before he did. As he opened the door, Briar and Jack could hear her say, "Take that jacket off - it's disgusting"

Briar didn't wait for them to drive off and shut the door, while they were still in the loading bay. The door didn't shut properly and Jack moved to take charge, but before he got to it, Briar had hip checked the door and it slammed shut.

"There's a knack," Briar said, as she bolted it shut.

"I got that," Jack offered. "You know I could take it off and sand it down, so there would be no need for barging." He walked over to the door to inspect it further
Briar glanced out at the shop and noticed a queue, "Great!" she offered as she headed up to the counter to serve. It took about 20 minutes for Briar to get rid of the queue and in that time, Jack had gone back upstairs and changed out of his jogging bottoms and in to a pair of jeans. Before the funeral order had been collected, Briar had asked for Jack to pop to the post office for her and collect a box, that was too big to be delivered by the normal postman.

Briar took the envelope of money out of her apron and stood behind the counter to count it. She glanced up to check there wasn't anyone waiting or, on a more sinister note, anyone that could try and grab the cash and try and run out of the shop. Briar had never thought about thieves in her shop until the charity collection tin had been nabbed and she had met her 'morning boys'. She finished counting. Having been given the right amount of money £300, she thought about the fact that she would be making another wad of cash in two days' time and it made her smile.

Jack skirted behind her and rested his warm hands on her hips. He leant round and kissed her left cheek. Briar shut the money in the till and placed her good hand on to his. She leant back into his body and their breath sync-ed up, they stood there not moving for about twenty seconds, enough time for all the towns busy bodies who were in the shop. Briar had counted three prevalent gossipers that morning to get a nice view of the new romance. Briar loved the fact that she didn't care about anyone looking at them. Jack remained where he was, but burst the bubble with the question, "Paperwork?"

"Don't move," she replied, closing her eyes and taking a deep breath.

"Come on, he said, squeezing her hips and moving to the side. Briar, who had let her whole body fall in to his, adjusted her centre of gravity and turned to face him. Briar dug out the slip of paper, that the postman had left for her, from her apron. A package had been left at central dispatch, all paid for, but it was too big to be delivered and needed to be collected. Jack, in his white knight status, was on his way to collect the package and needed the slip to get it, as his name wouldn't be on the collection list.

Jack took the slip and kissed Briar's nose, something she immediately disliked, and shouted, "Bye," as he grabbed his coat from inside the kitchen and headed out the front of the shop.

Briar stood there smiling at Jack as he left; she was idly rubbing her nose from where Jack had just kissed it. A couple had come up to the counter and the girl could see that Briar was in the middle of a swoon and waited to be noticed before ordering.

CHAPTER 11

The front door clanged open, with the back hitting the blue velvet armchair, startling Cleo the cat, who had been happily snoozing the afternoon away. She quickly shot through the kitchen and out the door like a bolt of lightning, to hide behind the bins of the shop next door.

A man was standing in the doorway. All that Briar could see from behind the counter was a pair of blue jeans and black trainers, but she knew immediately who the man was. It was her Jack. He was holding a brown box, that had a big arrow pointing to the ceiling. Briar was in the middle of her lunchtime rush and had just taken an order for a bacon roll and a pepper tea. She looked at the big figure letting in the draft.

Briar scanned across the busy shop, after hearing a lady tut loudly. She found Beret Lady staring at Jack; she had been sat frozen for the last couple of minutes, her tea cup poised about 6 inches from her lips, completely engrossed in what she was reading.

The lady, who had on a purple beret and far too many bracelets, finally put the tea cup down, after drinking the whole thing in one big gulp, returning to the page. She was reading one of the unpublished books, named 'Charlton.' and was at the crucial point where the book's heroine was about to inject herself with the death serum to save her sister from being attacked by the evil mastermind of the plot. And it was obvious from the tutting that she wasn't happy to be torn away from the story at such an exciting time.

Beret Lady, whom Briar was very surprised to see ever again, had ordered a tea and a cake as normal, but that day there had been no warmth in her voice. Briar had seen her walk past the shop window a couple of time, as if she was trying to build up enough courage to enter the shop. Briar had panicked slightly when she had seen Beret Lady, thinking that she might bring up the events of the day before again. But she placed her order, and went off to find a book without a hint of fuss. Briar was having an internal debate whether she should mention it, as she got her cake out the cabinet, but she decided that she was too chicken, and served her with a weak smile, a smile that had not been reciprocated.

Jack eased his way through the door, allowing it to close on the spring. Then stood there for a couple of seconds, trying desperately to remember a plot to get from the door to the counter, without knocking into any furniture and creating more of a commotion than he already had. The brown box was very heavy and in addition, he couldn't see over the top of it. As soon as he got through the door, he was feeling regret. 'If you had a couple more brain cells,' he said to himself, 'you could have taken them round to the kitchen door'. Jack felt Briar's right hand on his left one, as she said, "Ok, Step!"

Jack did as instructed and then felt pressure on his hand. "That way a bit," she continued to guide, as they edged through to the kitchen. Jack could feel eyes burning into the side of his head and his face started to go red.

As they got to the connecting door, Briar unlocked it and as Jack headed up the stairs with the box, she pinched his bum as he went through the door.

With the entrance of Beret Lady, Briar began to think of the potential suicide submission, that was currently sitting on top of the fridge next to the vase that contained all the roses. Jack hadn't disappointed Briar and had left a mint green rose next to the milk that morning. When Briar had opened, slightly later than normal due to the activities of the night before, Noel, one of her morning boys, had commented on the rose and when he had asked if 'the milkman' was her boyfriend, she had instinctively replied with a yes.

Briar grabbed the infamous novel from off the fridge and opened it up at the last page. Re-reading the suicide note, she flicked the kettle on and after a quick glance out to the shop, checked there was no one waiting or any mess to clear up. She flipped to the middle of the book, the part that she hadn't read, and began to try and piece together the content.

The tap is dripping. A woman, lying on her back in the bath, recalling the last five minutes of her life, has taken some sleeping pills and is slowly allowing them to take effect. She can feel the softness of her ex-foliated skin. She brings her knees up to her chest and looks at the white ceiling. She can see the window frosted up with steam and condensation running down onto the windowsill. As she closes her eyes, knowing that soon she would be fine, she would be in heaven with her family, she sees a shadow come over the bath believing that the pills are taking effect, she takes a big breath. The breath that she believes to be her last and the next thing she knows is she is waking up in a hospital bed with a tube coming out of her mouth. The shock of being alive hits her before the pain of her body living. The lights are bright, too bright and someone is holding her left hand running their fingers around her wedding ring finger in the playful manner. She could feel the cold metal against her skin. Her first thought after the initial, oh god I'm alive, was where am I?. Her second thought was who is holding my hand and why have I got a wedding ring on my finger. She slowly started to turn her head, letting out a small groan as

she did. 'Baby,' a man's voice echoed. "Baby I'm here". His voice was like butter. She turned to face him, her hazel eyes meeting his grey ones. There was worry showing around his forehead yet his mouth was smiling. "You are ok darling' you're at St Thomas' hospital."

Briar rubbed her eyes with her good hand before turning back to the book. 'What utter drivel she thought' her brain trying to make sense of the writing.

She groaned again trying to speak. The tube that went down her throat was getting more uncomfortable by the minute. She attempted to withdraw her hand from his grasp, but feeling so weak, she barely moved it 6inches. The man, however, didn't let go of her. The man she didn't recognise. She looked around wildly for someone else - someone that she knew, or a doctor, anyone who could help her but...

The clink of the front door was heard and Briar automatically looked up. A middle-aged couple walked in with a pram. She glanced back down at where she had been reading and saw the word 'alone.' She marked the page in the book with the top of an old card board box of loose tea. She had been using them as book marks for years and walked out of the kitchen to the counter. Briar was trying to understand the writing; she knew that it wasn't any good and that meant one of two things. I was one that it was from a person who had not sent in a submission before, as they had had nothing quite so bad, or it was someone who was intentionally writing in broken thoughts. Changing the gender of the victim and the tense of the writing.

Briar's good hand was casually placed comfortably in the pockets of her apron with her injured one still resting without a sling on her chest.

"Hello," she greeted them in a friendly manner. In reality, she was really enjoying trying to understand the book and rather reluctant to leave it, but customers paid the bills, and Briar knew that there was probably no danger to anyone and the 'Suicide note' was nothing more than the wrong end of the stick.

"Good morning", replied the woman, "could we please have a pot of tea for two and two slices of carrot cake?" Her smile radiated happiness. Briar instantly had a feeling of warmth towards the lady.

"Just one slice of cake," interjected the man, who was standing next to her. Briar had noticed that they had matching rings on and their baby looked exactly like his dad, but with the freckles and red hair of his mum.

"OK then, just one piece. Are you sure I can't tempt you to one of our other cakes?" she added, gesturing to the two shelves of cakes that were just behind the counter. "Maybe a chocolate or a scone perhaps?" said Briar, in a friendly manner. One thing that her mother always said was if you can get their tummy rumbling, they will always be happy.

"The carrot cake is for me," replied the man, "you're on a diet Geraldine, aren't you?" Briar's mouth slowly fell open. The way that he had casually put down his wife in front of a stranger was so rude that she could hardly get angry about it. The look of shock must have been written across her face. The lady, who by now had gone bright red, cleared her throat and asked for the tea to be 'Earl Grey please', and then, indicating a table, "we are going to sit over there." And then, grasping the pram with both hands, she sat down at a seat near the door, with her back to the counter and allowed the hair to fall in front of her face. Briar, having recovered from the insult, went straight to the till and rang up the order "£6.50," she said not meeting the eye of the gentleman. He went in his wallet and dug out a £50 note, handing it to her and looked nonchalant.

"Have you got anything smaller please?" inquired Briar, adding in a small smile.

"No," he replied meeting her smile with a creepy looking grin.

"Oh, OK, I will bring over your change with the tea." She had cashed up that morning and was all ready to go to the bank with the weeks' pay in.

She took the £50 to the safe, that was inside the pantry off the kitchen and exchanged it for some smaller change. As she came back, she had a sinister look on her face. Part of Briar was proud of herself for the fact that she had just sneezed over the carrot cake that she was going to serve to the creep. The other part of her was absolutely mortified at what she had done. She had never punished a person like that before - never messed with someone's food. The way that she had taken decisive action, and did it without really thinking about her actions, it showed a part to her character that she did not know she possessed. Briar's wrist hurt as she put the cake and the tea on the customers table. She looked at the clock in the kitchen, 11.47am, the thoughts of the shot of whiskey that was behind the sink for a second, as she popped a couple of pain killers in to her mouth and knocked them back with the cold blackcurrant tea that she had forgotten about, and now tasted like stale juice.

Briar sat down, flicked forward to another random page in the suicide novel and began reading.

I wonder how many people that have outstanding videos on their records are actually dead. As in they checked out the video on a Friday night for a weeks' rental and they died

before they could return it, maybe they even died before they could watch it. What a weird thing to think about! When you watch people for 10 hours a day, picking up something to watch, so you don't have to talk to your girlfriend or wife. you think of their lives that they have. Like Ernie he comes in every Friday night and rents an action film with a different girl every time. I think he just uses it as background noise to distract her, while he is trying to get her knickers off.

Briar took another sip of the cold tea, a quick glance in to the shop. The creep was eating the carrot cake. A smile spread over Briar's face and then the guilt crept back in. The text that she had been reading had stopped half way down the page and so she flicked it to the next one. Wondering what weird rambling would be next to read, she heard the thud on the stairs. Briar stared at the closed kitchen door, waiting for Jack to appear through it. She hadn't heard the stairs creak since her mum had been alive. With only Briar in the shop, there was never anyone in the flat alone. The knot appeared in her stomach and when she saw Jack, the butterflies joined in. Jack scanned the kitchen and when their eyes met, he smiled.

"Hi," he said in a very romantic movie over-the-top way, as he walked over to her.

"Hi," she replied, in an attempted romantic way; however, she didn't really pull it off.

"What's wrong?" asked Jack as he leant on the middle counter, where she had propped up the novel. "Wrist hurts?".

"I'm fine," replied Briar trying not to make a fuss, as she touched the bottom corner of the novel with the thumb of her good hand.

"I put the box in the living room and opened up the top," Jack informed her "Didn't want you arguing with the box cutter and slicing your other wrist," he added in a playful manner. Then he reached in to his back pocket and pulled out an envelope, which he put on the counter.

Briar read the front of the envelope. It read TUPTS. She looked at the acronym and smiled. Jack, bright as he was, hadn't quite got there and asked,

"Are you tupts?" not moving from his spot.

" No….well yes, 'The Unpublished Tea Shop'," she said, as she opened up the letter in the envelope. "It's a letter from the head of a writers group," Briar informed Jack, "In Scotland," she added. "They have," she began "Oh great….," Briar was talking and reading at the same time, "they have sent me forty novels for the shop"

"I carried forty novels?" Jack remarked. Then, without trying to sound modest, he added, "I didn't think I was that strong"

Briar folded the letter up and lobbed it onto the top of the fridge "That's next weeks' problem," she said, before looking back at the suicide novel. Mr Thompson was standing at the counter and, as Briar made a move to stand up, Jack walked round the counter and said, "I got this, you sit," before heading out to the front of the shop. Briar barely thought about arguing with Jack and turned her attention to the novel.

My head hurts because I want the ability to think. If I take my morphine, then I don't hurt, but I cannot make rational decisions. I can't process. I can't rely on me. So, my head is pounding. The red wine is breathing in the warm air. I have put a glass in the sun to warm, right on the edge of the wall, on uncle Donald's seat. I don't know why I always leave it

.

there, habit now I guess. His part of the wall is a bit more jagged than others, but I have never dropped a glass, never had a bottle spill. The history of our lives. The history that is encased in the wall. The honourable get granted grace, but me, I will not be discussed. I will fall from conversation and one day soon, my name will not be mentioned again.

"Do you charge for extra coleslaw?" Jack asked, breaking Briar's train of thought.

"No, but just one pot," she said, as she pointed to the fridge next to where Jack was standing. Briar bent down and grabbed a ramekin pot from under the microwave. Jack took the pot of coleslaw back out to the front and Briar re-read the passage in front of her.

She didn't move from her spot for the next twenty minutes, her mind flitting back to the suicide page on the back of the book and to other random chapters, that mentioned different characters, all centring on death and loss, but none of them connected to each other.

Briar finally looked over when Jack placed a cheese toasty in front of her. He had added a big dollop of coleslaw onto her plate and covered his toasty in what looked like tartar sauce.

"Thanks," she said, before opening the apology she had in her head. "I'm sorry that you have been running around after me all day," she added, taking a big bite out of her lunch.

"I enjoy helping you," replied Jack. "But," he continued, "if this is gonna be more of a permanent thing". Then he took a bite out of his lunch and began to chew.

Briar was feeling very nervous. What was he about to say, did he want paying? That would be fair for him to ask for a wage. Or, if he was gonna help maybe we should just be friends? Her mind was running at 100 miles an hour.

Jack finally swallowed the food and continued his statement "I'm gonna cancel my gym membership"

The air left Briar's lungs in a big sigh of relief, "Oh, right", she replied, not too sure how to use that information.

"Yeah it runs out next week," Jack elaborated, "if I'm gonna be here, which I love," he added, as his eyes met with Briar's "It's just a lot of money, if I'm not gonna use it every day". This wasn't meant as a dig to Briar, utilising so much of his time. Briar understood that and didn't take it personally.

Lunch was over quicker than either of them had wanted, however, with the lunch rush starting, they carried on through the afternoon, as if they had been together for years. At about 4pm, Carol popped in from the flower shop. Apart from thanking Briar for the scones, the only other thing she said was, "With him," gesturing to Jack, "you're not gonna need me for pee breaks anymore, are you?" but disappeared, with a smile on her face before Briar could answer her. Briar could see that Carol was very happy for her and not annoyed at getting ousted by a man.

By that evening, Jack and Briar were curled up on the sofa, watching an old film. She had cooked them mushroom risotto. Jack had popped to the off licence, down the road, for a bottle of wine, having to come back, the first time, to collect his ID, as the guy behind the counter, who 'looked 12,' had refused to serve Jack without seeing proof of age. Jack, who had served in the military for 7 years and had his car keys on him, had stomped back to the café to grab his driver's licence. Moaning the whole way, that the twelve year old behind the counter couldn't use his common sense, he wondered, how many seventeen year olds drive a Mercedes? The car was currently having a respray and Jack wasn't driving it at the moment, but that didn't matter. It was the principal of the thing and Jack believed that, with all the regulations, people were unable to think for themselves anymore. However, after a great dinner and the bottle of wine, Jack's mood was considerably high. The icing on the cake for him, was that Briar had fallen asleep on his shoulder and he had discovered, that she made this slight humming noise when she snored. Jack just sat there, drinking the last of his wine, watching the movie and smiling to himself how different his life had become in just five days.

CHAPTER 12- Friday

Working in the shop on Friday went by in a blink of an eye. What Briar remembered from the day, besides the pain in her arm, was the feeling of butterflies in her stomach, when she was around Jack. He had walked in after work with a huge bag of Chinese food, from the takeaway on the other side of town.

He had wanted to get food that Briar liked, however as they hadn't talked about Chinese food before. So, he had returned with seven main dishes and three types of rice. They had sat upstairs for three hours talking about everything from their first child hood memories to their favourite action hero.

Briar had brought the suicide novel upstairs when she had shut the shop up, however, with her focus being on Jack and the mountain of dinner he had arrived with. The novel sat on the coffee table and for the first time since that awkward conversation with Purple Beret Lady, Briar forgot about the knot in her stomach and the distress that the writer might already be in.

CHAPTER 13 - Saturday

Briar looked around the covered kitchen with delight; she cradled her wrist in her good hand, as she surveyed her accomplishment. On every surface, there was a cake or a tart of some description – Jack had even balanced a tray on the top of the two toasters, on which sat a chocolate crumble with hazelnut cream filling. The colours were bright and summery, and looked exactly the way she had planned, when she had taken the order from Mrs Hollis Jr three weeks earlier. Briar had put a fluorescent post-it note on the base of four of the desserts, as a reminder to dust them with icing sugar, just before they left the tea shop.

The morning rush was over, the shop was quiet and the customers were all eating and chatting happily, so she decided to treat herself to a cup of strong English Breakfast tea and a homemade chocolate biscuit. Jack was popping over to see his Mum and Dad, something he apparently did every Saturday. Jack had hinted that he might bring them over to the shop for a drink, something that hadn't been received that well by Briar. She was hoping that her reaction would persuade Jack to leave the parents at home. Not that Briar didn't want to meet Jack's Mum and Dad, it's just, that she did not want to meet Jack's Mum and Dad.

As Briar carefully dispensed the water in to her retro action figure mug, she glanced at the clock. It was 10.47am. Briar had been in the kitchen since just after 4. Jack had stayed over again and Briar had decided, she was going to get up and start baking when Jack left for work.

Briar glanced up at the front of the tea shop and noticed Purple Beret Lady, getting out her glasses to start reading. When she had served her earlier, she had tried to make conversation - it again hadn't gone well. Purple Beret Lady looked disappointed in Briar, and the knot that had arisen in her stomach, when she had been handed the suicide novel (as she was now calling it to herself), had only grown and now felt like a lump of concrete instead. Briar was starting to convince herself that it was a suicide note and with the line:

On this Holy day, it will seem to end quick. For my family, it will be a day burned into their memories.

Jack had rung the police and explained the situation, but they didn't seem to care very much. They had said that, when they could, they would send someone over to collect the novel. But the way Jack had said the officer had spoken, he didn't seem that worried and that it would be a couple of weeks before they would be able to analyse it.

Briar picked up the novel from on top of the fridge and began to look through it. She hadn't worked through the book in order and she was starting to wish that she had read the whole thing. But with the catering for the funeral and the party that week, with the addition of her injury and wanting to spend some time with Jack, it had been a very full week.

Briar believed that it was a person with gender identity issues, with the book beginning with her/him reference to themselves as a her. But another section discussed the entrance exam to a prominent boys' high school in the first person. A real school that was around eight miles out of the city centre, which meant that the author was local. Briar thought about her clientele, was there anyone who stood out? There was no other information on the novel about ownership and Briar had been tidying up, throwing away whichever packaging it had come in, when she unwrapped the new submissions on Monday.

As Briar poured a bit of milk in to her super hero mug, the hot liquid had changed the ridiculously attractive cast that were in their normal clothes in to action poses, covered in different coloured Lycra and ready to save the world from whatever evil villain was attacking their town that week. As she lifted up the glass milk bottle out of the fridge, she looked at the note that Jack had left for her. He had now moved on to writing full on words 'You're Pretty'. It made her smile. It turned out that Jack had been writing out a date proposal on milk bottles, one letter a bottle and not leaving any spaces between the words.

Briar got out a side plate and popped a biscuit from her special biscuit tin on the plate. This was her secret stash and she didn't make them often. Looking at the 'suicide note' on the last page, she bit into the cookie when there was a sharp rasp on the kitchen door. Briar glanced at the front of the shop, but as there was no one waiting there, she walked to the back of the kitchen, shoving the novel in her apron as she went. Munching away at the cookie, she had probably taken a bigger bite out of it than she should have done and was still chewing when she came face to face with the terrifying Mrs Hollis Jr.
Briar hip checked the kitchen door and opened it with quite a force. She was resting her bad hand on her boobs and had noticed that her top had slipped slightly and a bit of her red lacey bra was peeking out of the neckline.

"Hello," Briar said, trying to ensure none of the content of her mouth escaped.

"Good Morning," clipped Mrs Hollis Jr, "were you not expecting us at 11am?" in an equally worried and scolding tone. Briar decided to not point out that they were early and instead stepped back to reveal the cakes, allowing the reveal to be her reply. She stepped back, allowing the light to stream in to the kitchen. To say that it was the end of September, the weather outside was lovely, sadly one of the advantages of the melting ice caps. Briar thought to herself for a second, that Mrs Hollis Jr, with being so frosty, was probably helping balance out the environment.

There were two ladies flanking Mrs Hollis Jr. Briar watched them, as they scanned the array of desserts, and smiled to herself when both of their mouths dropped in awe of what she had created. The amazement on their faces only lasted a couple of seconds and luckily for both the worker bees, their queen didn't see their reaction,

"Right we are going to have to do a couple of trips I think" she said, gesturing to her ladies which trays to pick up first.

"I thought you said your son was collecting the food?" Briar asked, her hand still in front of her face

"Yes... well, obviously not," replied Mrs Hollis Jr, noticeably unhappy at the question. "Let's start with these", indicating the Viennese slices and the mint chocolate logs, "before we do the bigger ones".

Briar had not moved from her spot, this was something that she had learned after the mistake of last year, which resulted in Briar having to carry a couple of the cakes up to the Hollis house herself. The way that Mrs Hollis Jr had worded the question had resulted in Briar being unable to say no. Mrs

Hollis Jr lived on the same street as the shop, but she had come in her car. Briar believed that it was probably so that the less people saw her carrying desserts from the shop to her house, the better. Briar didn't believe that she would actively take credit for the desserts. If, however, the person didn't ask the question, she wasn't going to announce that she was not the cook.

Briar finished the last of the mouthful of cookie, which she had eaten without barely enjoying it, took a deep breath and adopted a power stance. The power stance only half worked. Having one injured hand, resting on her chest, she kind of felt that she was trying to show off her injury and stopped doing the power stance, before any of the ladies walked back in to the kitchen.

"Mrs Hollis," Briar began, "if we could sort out payment before you take everything please".

"I thought that I would send my son around with it later this evening," Mrs Hollis replied, roaming around the kitchen as if she owned it, inspecting the desserts as if she was looking for imperfections in the cakes.

"Oh, right then," Briar felt her nerve falter slightly. Another deep breath and she tried again, "It's just we agreed payment upon collection," trying to not feel like the entire body was the big knot in her stomach.

"I know we did, but I have been so busy organising anything", seeming as if she had not a care in the world, "sorting the flowers and the servers and not to mention the drinks that I had to re-order, because Mrs Greer cannot follow." Then with a big breath and a hint of terror in her eyes, "Simple instructions". Briar then watched as Mrs Hollis Jr spun round to face Briar, who was still standing next to the open door and stated, "I will send it round later". Briar wasn't sure, but she could have sworn that Mrs Hollis Jr's head had spun full circle.

"I mean, I am definitely good for the money," she said with a sly sideways smile.

Briar looked out to the front of the shop to see a customer coming through the door with a pram. Briar left the door open, avoided the smaller of the two ladies, who were loading the car up, and headed out to serve.

She recognised the lady immediately. It was the pretty red-head, this time without her horrid husband.

"How are you?" Briar greeted her warmly, trying to physically shake off the atmosphere that Mrs Hollis Jr. created whenever she was around. Briar thought that she may have to deep clean the place to scrub the creepy feeling away. It was either that or get the local reverend to come down and perform an exorcism. However, the unexpected arrival of a very happy looking Geraldine, had put a genuine smile on her face.

"What can I get you?" Briar asked, as she picked up a plate ready for her to hopefully name a cake that was full of calories.

"Can I have a latte please."

With a smile, Briar put down the plate and started to make the drink, trying to hide the slight sadness that had crept in. Was her husband still dictating what she could eat? Did she have to stand before him every night and give him a detailed run down of all the things she had eaten? Briar wanted to scream at this beautiful lady that she wasn't fat and shove a triple chocolate brownie down her throat.

"Have you had a nice day?" Briar asked trying to change the subject.

"Yes," she smiled rubbing her stomach idly, "I've just eaten at Russo's down the high road." She looked at the cakes, "those pasta bowls are lovely" and with that one statement, Briar felt a good foot taller.

Then suddenly there was a small crash followed by a squeal.

"Don't do that!" scolded Mrs Hollis Jr from the kitchen. The couple, who were having a very heated discussion, that looked half loving and half homicidal, stopped their fast talking and both stared through the open door into the back of the shop.

Briar finished pouring the latte and put it on the front counter.

"That should be right," offered Geraldine, as she held out her left hand with the money in it. At that moment, Briar noticed that her ring finger was bare. There was the tan line of where two rings had been when she had caught some sun, but now she wasn't wearing any jewellery. Briar couldn't hold her delight at the break down of a marriage. She watched as Geraldine weaved her way through the shop with the stroller, latte in hand. She sat down at the same table as last time. She took her child out of the stroller and sat him on her lap.

Briar remembered that there had been a squeal and headed in to the kitchen to investigate. She was hoping that one of the other ladies had accidently pied Mrs Hollis Jr and now she had a hair full of cream. This lovely thought evaporated immediately when she saw all three ladies and not a hair out of place between them. There were two meringue nests on the floor in front of the ladies, none of them had tried to clean up the mess that they had made.

"There was a noise," said the shorter of the two ladies, trying to sound as cold as their fearless leader, but unfortunately, she hadn't pulled it off. At Briar's stance, with her hand on her hip and the scowl that was all over her face, the short lady picked up another tray and headed out to the car.

"A noise made you jump?" Briar stated, as she went for the dustpan and brush. "It was only the oven.......not an air horn," she spat the words at the women. In truth, it was the oven turning off after cooking a blueberry sponge cake that Briar had forgotten she had made.

"And how many of them broke?" she enquired, as she gathered up the discarded food from the floor. Briar tone seemed to change the mood of the room, and she could see that everyone could feel it.

"Just two," Mrs Hollis Jr replied, trying to maintain a look of control on her face "The rest are packed in the car". She tried to pass it off, as if it had not been insulting to drop something that had taken Briar a good three hours to make and not even apologise.

"I think if Minnie and I walk up with these two trays, we will get the rest in the front seat of the car," Mrs Hollis Jr. added, asserting her self-imposed superiority. "Maggie can drive up to the house." She looked around the room to check that no trays, other than the ones on the central counter, remained.

Briar assumed that Maggie was the taller of the two ladies. She had gone pale and her shoulders were around her ears. Maggie's hands were clasped in front of her and her knuckles were white from how hard they were grasping each other. Briar assumed that it had taken quite a lot to become one of Mrs Hollis Jr's inner circle. Crashing a car and wrecking all the desserts, on what is the social event of the season for

Mrs Hollis Jr, would put her not only on the outside of the circle, but would probably leave her with no friends.

"Ok then", said Mrs Hollis Jr, "it looks like we are all sorted" Her eyes actively avoided the area where the mess had been, just in case Briar had failed to tidy it all up.

Briar looked at Maggie and saw that she was letting herself be manipulated as much as the old lady. We agreed on payment upon collection, Briar thought to herself.

"Actually," Briar began, her head running so fast that she was finding it hard to form a sentence, "I am going to need payment now" She was leaning her bum on the counter, as she adjusted her wrist before walking over to the open kitchen door.

"I said that I would bring it over tomorrow," Mrs Hollis Jr retorted, squaring up to Briar in a very lady like manner.

"We agreed on payment upon collection," countered Briar. She could see that there was a man waiting to be served, but her instinct and pride wouldn't let her lose this battle.

"Unfortunately, I don't have the cash on me." She made a step towards the door.

"I will happily take a cheque," Briar countered her step and moved one step sideways, to remain in front of Mrs Hollis Jr. The two ladies remained still for couple of seconds, weighing each other up.

"As you wish," she conceded, as she put her pale blue handbag on the counter and snapped open the clasp. The little air that was in the room, seemed to be sucked out completely. Putting the cheque book on the counter, she seemed to write it very slowly. The queue was getting longer in the front of the shop, but Briar couldn't bring herself to stop witnessing this victory she was currently experiencing.

"Ok, then," Mrs Hollis Jr tore the cheque off from the page, "it looks like we are all sorted here." Her eyes actively avoided Briar's stare. She motioned to the other lady to pick up the heavier of the two trays and she headed outside.

"Bye," offered Briar, as she checked the amount for the food was correct. £600 would go in the bank and the concrete in her stomach did a little somersault.

Briar turned to see the two ladies staring at the one in the car, as she backed it out of the loading bay. Remembering the queue, she quickly shut the door, hip checking it closed, and headed off to serve.

The smile remained spread across her face for the next hour.

CHAPTER 14

It was after three before Briar laid eyes on Jack. It had been a rather slow afternoon. With the Hollis Party starting at 4pm, a lot of her customers had popped in earlier, or not at all, to allow themselves enough time to get ready for the party.

Briar had forgotten to add the rest of the sugar flowers to the cakes when she dusted them with icing, so she decided to try and do a fancy display cake with the Blueberry sponge, that she had forgotten about earlier that day. She was adding the last flower to the base of the cake, when she felt Jacks arms around her.

"Hello," she said, as he nuzzled is face into her neck, smelling the papaya and coconut of her hair from the shampoo. Jack had done a good job of tying her hair up that day, better than what he had done the day before. Briar had had to ask a customer that she sort of knew, to step in and braid her hair, so that it wouldn't fall out. It had only cost her a couple of scoops of chocolate mint ice cream to get the girl to help her.

"How was your lunch?" Briar asked, stopping the arranging and allowed herself to be cuddled.

"It was fun," answered Jack, in a half coherent tone, "Harry got engaged"

"Your brother Harry?" Briar half asked and half checked that she knew who he was referring to.

"Yep," said Jack. Briar could tell that Jack didn't seem overly thrilled about the engagement.

"What's up?" she asked, as she leant further into the embrace

"I have to move out," whispered Jack. Briar's whole body became tense and she was cold with sweat.

Jack reacted to the fact that he felt like he was now hugging a tree and released his embrace. Briar turned to face him, as she reiterated, "You have to move out"

"Yep." He moved a strand of hair from in front of her face and hooked it behind her ear. "End of the month. Harry wants to put it on the market so that he can pay for the wedding"

Briar made a noise that was a cross between an oh and a what.

Jack changed the subject, "Hey, someone stole all the food!"

"Picked up this morning," remarked Briar, before she added, "paid in full".

"That's great," replied Jack. Briar knew that he didn't really understand the triumph of getting one over on Mrs Hollis Jr and she didn't really want to explain it to him.

Briar thought about her breath smelling and being so close to Jack. She had had a bit of whiskey when Carol had popped in unexpectedly and she had been used for a pee break. Briar had gone to the loo and then wandered in to the kitchen and taken a shot of whiskey from the bottle, before she had thought about what she was doing.

Briar had known that Carol had been up half the night as well, as she was providing the flowers for Mrs Hollis Jr's event, and after she had come down from her break, Briar had given her a bowl of chilli and a coffee muffin to go home with.

Briar wanted to talk about the housing situation, as she felt the concrete knot in her stomach getting bigger. She picked up one of the spare sugar flowers and held it at Jack's mouth. He opened it and she placed it on his tongue before he ate it whole.

"So, where are you gonna live?" Briar asked trying to keep her voice even.

Before Jack could answer, the front door of the shop opened, and Briar walked through to the front to serve.

Briar watched as Charlotte, the girl that had collected the funeral platters a couple of days previously, walked in. This time, she had on a blue and green pin striped dress with two large pockets in the front of it. Over the top of it, she was wearing a man's black jacket with a red cross sewn in to the back. Briar thought that she had seen the jacket before, but couldn't place it.

Briar watched as she walked slowly to the counter, looking as though she was trying to kill as much time as possible.

"Good afternoon," Briar greeted her warmly, hoping that she wasn't there to complain about the food she had prepared.

"Hi," replied Charlotte, with a weak smile that seemed to mask the look of annoyance for a second, before returning to her previous facial expression.

"What can I get you?" asked Briar, her good hand hovering in mid-air between the serving plates and cups.

"Do you do baked potato?" asked Charlotte, placing her hands in the jacket before finding something that she wasn't expecting and removing her hand and putting it on the counter. She tried to conceal the look of shock as Briar answered.

"Yeah of course," Briar said trying to not sound too enthusiastic as there was no complaint, as she added, "It will take about thirty minutes to cook."

"Fab," she replied, handing over a £10 note.

Briar rang it up before asking, "Which filling?" and pointing to a chalk board behind the mug stack.

"Coleslaw......and a glass of tap water please"

Briar thought to herself that she hadn't even asked about a drink - that was very unlike her.

Handing over her change and the water, she instructed Charlotte, "Take a seat and I will bring your food over"

"No rush," Charlotte offered.

Briar tried to keep a distance with customers, but the girl didn't look in pain as such, more the need to vent, so she asked,

"You ok?"

"Fine, just so many old people. I feel like they try and suck the life out of you sometimes."

Briar laughed "Where have you been?"

"Michaelmas celebration," Charlotte replied

"What's that?" Briar asked, hoping she didn't sound stupid.

"Mrs Hollis', a Christian party that she throws every year. We only went this year because my gran died."

"Oh right," said Briar, still not understanding why she had gone

"They unveiled a plaque on the wall, outside her house, with gran's name on, so, we had to go,". Charlotte added. "Gran always said one of the big bonuses' of being Muslim was that you didn't get invited to Michaelmas"

"Bet it's not too bad a party" Briar said, with a cheeky smile, "I hear the cakes are good".

"My friend said he would be there, but he won't come out of his room and my grandad said I couldn't go and get him," Charlotte added, "so I left".

"Aren't there any other younger people there?" asked Briar.

"No, I think only Carl gets to come because he is her son."

Briar then clocked whose coat that was. It was Carl's. She had seen the back of it when they were loading the funeral food into the car. Briar then felt a pang of guilt. He was keeping his back hidden from view, as Briar had forgotten to tell any of the waiter candidates the outcome of the interview.

Charlotte smiled and walked over to one of the big arm chairs. Placing the jacket on the arm, she sat down and got her phone out.

Briar walked in to the pantry and grabbed a big potato from the basket. Jack was sitting where Briar had been when she was decorating the cake. Jack however was on his phone.

"So where do you think you're gonna live?" Briar asked, as she stabbed the potato with a big knife that she was securing with the crook of her arm.

Jack didn't look up to answer Briar, "There are a couple of to-lets down the street that look good".

Briar was starting to get annoyed that she was talking to the crown of his head. As she walked past him to put the potato in the microwave, she noticed that he was looking at houses, and the concrete knot got a bit smaller.

As Briar walked passed Jack, back to the front of the shop, he grabbed her jeans at the waist and pulled her into him.

"I took a walk up the street," he said, as she moved in to his personal space, "I was just sorting out a viewing for tomorrow.....Wanna come?"

"Which one?" asked Briar, not that that was a deal breaker she thought, anything would be good.

"The one opposite the big house at the bottom," he replied with a little head gesture to the bottom of the street.

Briar knew that the house he was talking about was Mrs Hollis Jr's and she didn't like the idea that she may run into that awful woman, if Jack got the flat, but she wanted to be supportive.

"Great," Briar responded. She was hoping that she would sound enthusiastic and reminded herself that she needed to make up the plate for the jacket potato.

"It was all cracking off today, down there," Jack said. He sensed that Briar wanted to be released from his embrace and obliged her.

"It's the party that they collected for," Briar explained, as she began to sort out Charlotte's plate.

Briar had left the suicide novel propped open and Jack, whose phone had died, had started reading it.

He tried to turn the page, but with the weight of the paper, it flipped to the back page. Jack sat reading, thinking he should, as Briar had bought it up a couple of times and the book being out, meant that she was still thinking it was something to worry about.

Jack read the note on the back page. Briar was serving a customer and he went through to the front counter. Once the man had walked away, Jack offered, "This is some heavy stuff!"

Briar leant on the counter, "Yeah, hopefully, it's just a prank"

"All the angles," he said, looking down at the page, "Shakespeare as well"

"I know Cleopatra"

".....And the sonnet," Jack pointed to the back page

"Oh!" Briar walked over and stood with Jack, her arm resting on his hip bone. She hadn't realised it was a sonnet, just that it was a poem.

"Sonnet 71 – it's my favourite"

This life has taken the soul out of me and I shall

No longer mourn for me when I am dead

"That's why I have it tattooed on my back," Jack expressed, still sitting on Briar's stool.

Briar became instantly embarrassed. She didn't know he had a tattoo on his back.

"It's said to be a favourite among scholars and soldiers," Jack offered "Its saying I created this when I'm alive, so don't mourn for me when I'm dead…….. It's a goodbye."

Briar froze on the spot, thinking about the number 71. She had seen it before, but couldn't remember where. Then Briar thought about Charlotte sitting in the shop. All angels….. Michaelmas. It was today, it was happening today.

"What's wrong babe?" asked Jack. He was looking at her wrist, trying to see if there was any blood coming through the bandage.

But Briar wasn't listening to him. She was thinking about the middle part of the book, with the red wine on the wall and the plaques for the honoured people of the town……

CHAPTER 15

Briar tore out of the shop at full speed. Her apron strings were coming loose behind her and Jack was quick on her heels; however, being a former athlete and very quick on his feet, he started to pull ahead of Briar. But as he didn't know what was happening, he slowed to keep pace. They were halfway down the street before they heard the front door to the shop clink shut. They had left a full shop of customers and the till had over three hundred pounds in it. There were orders that were waiting to be filled and defiantly three rashes of bacon under the grill that Jack was going to eat. But none of that mattered. Briar's sole focus was getting to Carl. Jack had slowed up slightly and was now running parallel to Briar. She banged on the white front door with an open palm. "Hello?....Carl.... Mrs Hollis. Hello?" she shouted loudly.

Jack was crouching down, trying to see through the thick net curtain into the living room. He looked up and shook his head.

Briar's whole face lit up as she spluttered, "Servants entrance" and ran past Jack and along the old wall.

In between the old plaques, that looked weather worn, was a shiny new one that had been decorated with a single lily. It was a large Manor House and Briar knew that the kitchen was near to the back garden.

Briar got round to the back of the house and hopped over the 5 foot gate, something she managed to do even with her wrist on her chest. Jack also cleared the wrought iron gate, however with a lot more grace, unintentionally showing off his athletic physique. They were running up a small twitchel that was full of moss. It had barely been used since the Manor House had housed servants and they were required to enter the building in a discreet way. Briar and Jack's pace was steady and they made it to the end of the twitchel in less than 10 seconds. Briar had been down the twitchel once, when she was a child and had accepted a dare to find out, what colour the servant's door was. It was black. They made it to the door and as the momentum force of them running hit the door it opened and knocked into a table. There were caterers arranging platters, who barely got to glance at them, before they whizzed up the stairs to the main point of the house. Jack, who still didn't know what was happening, was following Briar's lead and was less than a second behind her the whole time. As they reached the entrance hall, the party was in full swing. Mrs Hollis Jr whom had been in conversation with a couple of overdressed gentleman stared at Briar with a look of horror.

"What?" she began

"Carl where is Carl?" Briar screamed at her, tentatively cradling her wrist which was in agony.

"Who?" asked Mrs Hollis Jr, as if she had never heard the name before

"Your Son, Carl!" Briar replied, her voice still at the same high pitch.

"He is in his room"

Briar tore up the grand staircase

Mrs Hollis Jr. turned from Briar to Jack, who had followed her up the stairs. The commotion that they had created had caused the room to fall silent and everyone was now looking at the space that had been occupied by Briar and Jack a few moments earlier.

"So sorry for the interruption" Briar heard Mrs Hollis Jr offer in a way of an apology to her guests and the murmuring and clinking of glasses resumed.

CHAPTER 16

The front door clinked shut behind her. Briar didn't glance back at the crowd of people she had just walked through in front of the shop. She didn't know how long they had been standing outside. She didn't know how long it had been since running out of the shop. When did they leave their tea and cakes to watch the scene that was developing at the bottom of their quiet, little street? Was it when the police car arrived? Or the Ambulance? She didn't wonder what she looked like and ignored the mirror that was over the hearth as she passed it. She stood in front of the counter and turned to face people for the first time in what felt like an age. As she did, she noticed the burnt bacon on the side smouldering still in its pan. She stared at it for a couple of seconds taking time to process the events. The bacon had obviously been removed by a customer, but no one came forward for praise and she didn't bother to ask. People were muttering, curious to know the reason why the owner of one of the most famous independent tea shops in the county, had flown out of the door. Ten seconds earlier, everyone had been absorbed in their own problems and thoughts, being under the impression that everything was plodding along nicely.

Briar cleared her throat, attempted a power stance and asked in the biggest voice she could master, "the tea shop is closed. I'm sorry for the inconvenience. If you could all please collect your things. I have got"...her nerve faulted and she lost her words.

But Jack metaphorically caught her and continued," there are paper containers and cups to have the rest of your purchases at home," and with that, he put a strong hand around Briar's shoulder and guided her through the maze of people, up the stairs leaving a muttering of noise behind them both.

She had a bit of blood smeared on her face. Jack was unsure if she knew about it. Jack was fully aware of the amount of blood both on her and himself. He was doing a very good job of hiding how squeamish blood made him feel. He took her upstairs and sat her on the sofa. Briar was looking round the room, the shock of the last 30 minutes was starting to set in. He returned about five minutes later with a cold can of pop from the fridge downstairs. He opened it and the sound of the can made Briar stand up, but he was there, beside her, before she could take a step. "Here drink this," he ordered softly, as he slowly sat her back down.

"The shop?" she enquired after necking half the can in a single gulp.

"All locked up," he assured her. He moved so he was facing her. Crouched, as if he was about to leap frog over a post, he began to undue the laces on her shoes and eased them off.

"I...," Briar tried to vocalise any of the thousand thoughts that was going through her brain, but she couldn't form the words.

Jack had already removed her socks and his own shirt that was doused in blood. He was careful to place it on the wooden floor and not the carpet rug. Briar trusted Jack, if not before today, then the events showed what kind of man he was and she allowed him to manipulate her clothes.

Only when he took hold of her elbows and softly said "Stand up", did she enquire as to what he was doing. "You're gonna have a shower. Get you all clean".

Briar glanced down at his hands softly cupping her elbows and that is when she noticed. She was almost completely covered in blood. It was spattered on her jeans. At some point she had lost her apron. Her light grey tank top was drenched and there was dried blood on both of their hands and her bandaged wrist.

"Oh God!" she cried on an out breath.

"It's ok, you are OK" Jack comforted her.

" I should have done something, I.....I should have. I should have been able to.....," She replied.

Jack didn't try and explain that she had done something, that they were the ones that were there. He let her sob and after a short while, he led her in to the bathroom and stood just outside, with the door open, and allowed her to stand in the bath until the shower water ran cold.

The End

Stories are always arriving in the tea shop. Read on to discover what is in store for Briar.

When coming in to the tea shop you can sit and read for hours. Today there is a smell of icing sugar in the air and freshly ground coffee. Glancing in to the corner of the shop there is a table, where three friends had left some books that they had been reading, whilst devouring a huge slice of Victoria sponge.

Noisy Neighbours

The mist settled in the air over the graveyard, it was November and the cold weather had taken hold on central London and had begun to squeeze the colour out of the city. The wind picked up and the cloud quickly passed over Mount Hope Graveyard and the moon shone on the two freshly dug graves. The right occupant was Martin Cooper, quoted on his headstone to be a loyal husband and son to Toby, Cory and Oliver. He was a London banker and when his children had to put down their father's job title they always managed to misspell banker with a W.

The black marble on the lavish head stone was cold to touch. The red roses that had been left there from the funeral two days previous had died in the cold. The petals that had not left the stem for the floor had stuck themselves to the expensive marble.

The resident next door was a lady named Queenie Holt. She was the daughter to a Jamaican mother and a Russian father. She had lost her only daughter in a house fire when she was 22 and had raised her granddaughters from the age of three until they had buried her two days previously. Helena and Hermia were named after Shakespeare's characters in the dream play. Queenie had always referred to the twins as her Dream Babes. When the Granddaughter's had buried her, they had matching tattoos covered in cling film that read 'Though she be but little she is fierce'. This was the quote that they had decided to engrave on her head stone to match the tattoo and forever connect the twins to Queenie.

With the date of death and a scheduling fau par the funerals had taken place at the same time side by side. Martins family all wore black, their expressions as cold as the weather, the catholic priest droned on in a monotone voice about how he was a pillar of the community. During the service three men checked their watches to see if it was nearly over.

Queenie's service was a lot more colourful, with the mourners wearing sunflowers on their lapels. The air seemed warmer on that side of the Graveyard, no one had checked their watches and the Reverend recalled a story when Queenie had chased a pigeon out of the church kitchen with a bible before a coffee morning.

The Weaver

The telegram arrived at 4pm sharp. The post boy wasn't used to delivering telegrams to such a rundown area of Manchester. The back to back housing was full of children with runny noses and grazed knees. As he walked up to number 44 he checked the house number again. He didn't want to disturb the wrong person, as he knew this area of Manchester didn't react kindly to strangers.

"Errol, Errol" boomed a voice from behind the door.

The post boy stepped back and braced himself for the man who was heading to the door. The surprise that was written across the boy's face when a small, formidable looking woman answered the door and stated, "You're not Errol".

"No" he replied, grasping the telegram in his right hand as he held it at arm's length towards the woman.

"Oh, lovely" sounding both happy and annoyed at the same time. She slammed the door and walked back towards the kitchen. Opening the telegram and walking towards the light coming through the kitchen window. If she had looked out the window she would have seen the post boy running down the street as fast as his legs would have taken him. But she didn't worry about post boys. She read the letter using her left eye as that hadn't been claimed by diabetes as yet.

"Two please. Four PM tomorrow. The Warden"

She crumpled up the telegram and threw it on the fire. There was a weathered wooden box next to the hearth, she sat in front of it and flipped it open. Rubbing her callused hands on her apron before she picked up the rope twines and beginning to wrap them together.

The old lady sat there for about two hours before she stood up to poke the coals in the fire. As she did she threw the rope on the table. The noose that she had just finished tying landed with a thud.

The back door opened and the man announced himself with a large belch.

"You disgusting pig" the lady spat at him.

"Someone is gonna die then" as he slammed the door and sat down at the kitchen table.

Briar picked up the novels and put them in her new apron, throwing a tea towel over her shoulder as she gathered the crockery. Leaning forward, at that precise moment, if you were to look at the happy owner. You would have seen the outline of the baby bump hidden beneath her shirt.

28438986R00102

Printed in Great Britain
by Amazon